Jane Ellison was born in Dewsbury, Yorkshire, and educated at Sheffield High School for Girls and Girton College, Cambridge, where she read Classics. For the past ten years she has worked as a journalist, notably for *Vogue* and the *Standard*, and currently for *Private Eye*. She is married and lives in London.

Author photograph by Roy Cook

A Fine Excess

Jane Ellison

BLACK SWAN

A FINE EXCESS

A BLACK SWAN BOOK 0 552 99228 3

Originally published in Great Britain by
Martin Secker & Warburg Ltd.

PRINTING HISTORY

Martin Secker & Warburg edition
published 1985
Black Swan edition published 1986
Reprinted 1986

This book is set in 11/12 pt Mallard
compugraphic by Colset Private Limited,
Singapore.

Black Swan Books are published by
Transworld Publishers Ltd., 61 – 63
Uxbridge Road, Ealing, London W5 5SA, in
Australia by Transworld Publishers (Aust.)
Pty. Ltd., 15 – 23 Helles Avenue, Moorebank,
NSW 2170, and in New Zealand by
Transworld Publishers (N.Z.) Ltd., Cnr.
Moselle and Waipareira Avenues,
Henderson, Auckland.

Made and printed in Great Britain by the
Guernsey Press Co. Ltd., Guernsey, Channel Islands.

To P.G.C.

Acknowledgments

My thanks are due to the following for permission to quote from published material:

Lines from

'Nemea VII' by Pindar are taken from *The Odes of Pindar*, translated by Richmond Lattimore, © 1947 by the University of Chicago, and are reproduced by kind permission of The University of Chicago Press, Chicago, Illinois.

The Cocktail Party by T.S. Eliot are reproduced by kind permission of Faber and Faber Limited, London.

'I Cain't Say No', music by Richard Rodgers, words by Oscar Hammerstein II, © 1944 Williamson Music Inc., are reproduced by kind permission of Williamson Music Limited, London.

'Tea for Two', music by Vincent Youmans, words by Irving Caesar, © 1924 Harms Inc., are reproduced by kind permission of Chappell Music Limited, London.

J.E.

ε᾽ίρειν στεφάνους ἐλαφρόν· ἀναβάλεο· Μοῖσά τοι
κολλᾷ χρυσὸν ἔν τε λευκὸν ἐλέφανθ᾽ ἁμᾷ
καὶ λείριον ᾽ανθεμον ποντίας ὑφελοῖσ᾽ ἐέρσας.

Pindar
Nemea VII

*Lightly will I make garlands. Strike up now. For you the
  Muse
binds gold upon white ivory with
the lily growth, raised dripping from the sea.*

Translated by Richmond Lattimore

Poetry should surprise by a fine excess,
and not by singularity;

Keats
To John Taylor,
27 February 1818

1

One bright day in October three poets set out to keep an appointment in the dismaying heart of London. They were all famous in an unimportant way; a selection of their work appeared in Modern British Verse, an anthology widely read in secondary schools. But probably no more than six people in all the world could remember a line of their poetry.

Coming from different directions the poets negotiated the traffic with confusion or skill, according to their dispositions. Two of them arrived simultaneously at their destination which was Fussell's Hotel, a cause for wonder and surprise in Wormald Square. Cream and rose brick, it stood ten storeys high and decorative flags flew from its ingenious turrets. The elder of the two, Howard Antick, imaginatively supposed that the flags were the proud banners of the nations of the world, but in this he was mistaken. They flew in honour of the package tour companies whose clients regularly stayed at Fussell's.

The two poets recognised each other in the foyer which was dimly lit and dismal. Cleaning machines were stacked by the entrance to the restaurant and there was dust on the vestibule's marble fireplace.

'Good to see you, Howard,' said Gavin Jarvis, a leading younger poet. 'Glad you could make it.'

'It wasn't far,' said Howard Antick. 'Further for you to come, much further. Did you have difficulties with the trains?'

'I came on my bike,' said Gavin Jarvis.

'Motor bike?'

'Kawasaki.'

'Splendid,' said Antick insincerely.

The poets went to the Rembrandt Room. They examined its proportions. Designed to circumscribe private banquets, its green-papered walls extended emptily around a circular table which had been set for lunch. Dirty curtains obscured windows through which passing cars cast momentary shadows. A pile of hard-backed chairs was stacked in one corner.

'Violet is late,' said Howard Antick. 'We can't start without her.'

Seeing the arrangements of the wine glasses Antick felt his spirits rise. He thought of the days of his youth when he had been invited to a private lunch party for T. S. Eliot and the great poet had asked him for a cigarette.

He turned to Gavin Jarvis. 'All this reminds me of the day I had lunch at T. S. Eliot's table in Buntings in 1935.'

Jarvis blew cigarette smoke in Antick's face.

'Of course, I was just a young scribbler then,' said Antick, 'but it made the most tremendous impression on me, the way Eliot leaned forward and said, "I wonder if you could let me have one of your cigarettes," His voice, I remember, was most unusual. It was the tone, the resonance that struck me as something quite remarkable. I must say I realised then that I was in the company of a man of genius, great genius.'

Gavin Jarvis said nothing.

'How often,' Antick continued, 'does genius seem beyond our comprehension. Indeed we hardly know how to define it. And yet, there I was with a man who seemed to announce in his everyday speech that he was possessed of an exalted vision, a vast, creative imagination, while, of course, saying the most ordinary things. The point about him,' said Antick, 'was that –'

A waiter came into the Rembrandt Room and asked them if they wanted a drink.

'Light ale,' said Jarvis.

'OK sir,' said the waiter.

'– that his remarks were always quite original. It is important to remember the exact words – the *ipissima verba* –,' said Antick, 'because only then can you grasp the essential character of the man. However, if memory serves me right –'

'Aperitif?'

'– he leaned forward and asked me, a total stranger indeed – for he did not know me from Adam – if I could let him have a cigarette. Yes, yes, he said, "I wonder if you could let me have a cigarette," though I certainly had not been introduced to him and I –'

'Do you want a drink?' said Jarvis, making drinking movements with his hand.

'Whisky and soda,' said Antick hastily. 'Large one.'

The waiter disappeared.

A photographer came into the Rembrandt Room carrying a canvas bag, an apparatus of flash lights and a silver folding umbrella.

'Poetry judging?' he said.

'We are the judges, yes,' said Antick, 'for the Coote & Balding Poetry Competition. Quite right, yes, do come in.'

'Cheers,' said the photographer encouragingly.

'This is the photographer from the press,' Antick said to Jarvis. 'He has come to photograph us, the judges.'

'I know,' said Garvin Jarvis.

'Let me explain the arcane mysteries of our ceremony,' Antick said to the photographer. 'First of all we shall take luncheon, then we shall subsequently discuss the merits of our short-listed poems. Finally we shall make our decision, difficult though that may be. Rest assured we shall find our winner and declare him. Indeed, we may find it an easier task than we have supposed. We may be –' and Antick lowered his voice dramatically, '– we may be unanimous in our verdict.' He laughed abruptly. Jarvis and the photographer regarded him in some alarm as his laughter precipitated a prolonged fit of coughing.

'If you're shooting profiles,' Jarvis said to the

photographer, 'could you do me a favour and take me from the left. It's my best side they tell me.'

'Up to you, squire,' said the photographer. 'Whichever side you like.'

The waiter appeared with a tray of drinks. Greedily Antick stretched out a quivering hand to take his whisky. Then he noticed the photographer. 'I say,' he said, 'would you care for a drink?'

'Not for me,' said the photographer.

'Not even a Perrier?' said Jarvis.

'Not while I'm working. You go ahead.'

'That is impossible,' said Antick, gulping his whisky. 'One of our number is missing. Nothing can be done without her. I mean Violet Glasspool, author of *Orisons* and *An Unmown Meadow*.' Antick's grey hair fell in disarray over his parchment forehead. 'Perhaps one of us should telephone?' he said excitedly. 'She may have mistaken the date or worse, met with an accident on the way here.'

'Violet is never on time,' said Jarvis with authority.

'Oh, you know that, do you?' said Antick.

'Yes.'

'Well, well, well,' said Antick. 'Splendid.'

For some minutes they drank in silence as the photographer built pyramids of electric lights.

'I found myself entering the Gents,' said Violet Glasspool, suddenly coming into the Rembrandt Room. 'I saw, for a second, the spectacle of men unzipping themselves before my eyes. I've been wandering round this horrible place for hours and hours. Howard, my dear, how are you? It's a positive labyrinth. Gavin, darling, I'm terribly late.'

'Why didn't you ask at reception?' said Gavin Jarvis.

'What was reception?' said Violet Glasspool. 'I couldn't find anyone to ask. I'm horribly flustered.' She stared at them through her thick spectacles in an agitated manner.

'Violet, my dear,' said Howard Antick, moving slowly towards her. 'Let me take your mackintosh.' As he

14

removed her coat the odour of her perspiration slowly filled the room.

'I'm so sorry,' she said. 'I thought you might have started.'

'Ah no,' said Antick. 'You see, that would have been quite improper. Clearly against the rules. We are taking aperitifs. Will you have something, Violet?'

'Well, I don't know if I should,' said Violet Glasspool, lowering her eyes. She was the kind of woman who had to be coaxed into drinking in public. Gallantly they did their best.

'Oh well, a dry sherry,' she said at last. 'But just a little one.'

'And another whisky and soda,' said Antick, 'large, no ice.'

The photographer put up his silver umbrella, then he began to walk round the room, inspecting its dusty recesses. The poets tried to ignore him. A fourth man came into the Rembrandt Room unnoticed. He was Hubert Bacon, representative of Coote & Balding, tobacconists to the Queen and generous sponsors of the national Coote & Balding Poetry Competition. Bacon had been chosen for the job of supervising the judges because of his flair for humorous verse, which he had contributed to the Coote & Balding house magazine, *Filter Tipped*, for the last fifteen years. It was felt at Coote & Balding House that his poetic talents would equip him for any possible display of artistic temperament from the judges. Nervously he approached them.

'Hubert Bacon,' he said. 'You're all here? Very good. I can see you're getting to know each other. Have you all the drinks you want?'

The poets regarded him with some doubt.

'I am the man from Coote & Balding,' said Bacon modestly.

'You want what is known as reception,' said Howard Antick, whose hearing was defective. 'It's in the vestibule. May I show you the way?'

'No, Howard' said Gavin Jarvis. 'This is Hubert Bacon, the man who's paying the bill.'

15

'So sorry,' said Antick, retreating nervously. 'So very sorry. I didn't quite catch . . . a thousand apologies.'

Bacon extended a hand to Jarvis who shook it languidly. As the sponsor breathed a welcome, Jarvis noted the fumes upon his breath. Unknown to them all, Bacon had been in the Rubens Bar since mid-morning, fortifying himself against the coming ordeal.

'I suggest we might begin lunch,' said Bacon, 'before advancing to higher things.'

'Splendid,' said Antick. 'We shall certainly fulfil our tasks better on a full stomach.' A veteran of poetry competitions, he had high expectations of Coote & Balding hospitality. A company as rich as they would surely furnish them with lavish spoils. Approvingly, Antick eyed the embossed silver cutlery, the stiff napkins and the crested china. The poets followed Bacon to the table in single file.

'Do we bring our files with us to lunch,' said Violet Glasspool, 'or are we not allowed to talk shop yet?'

'Dear me,' said Antick, in a high, excited voice, 'let us concentrate on our food. One of the great pleasures of life and let no one be ashamed to admit it. Second only perhaps to poetry or fine wine. Or women,' he added, as an afterthought.

'Poor old Antick,' Gavin Jarvis said softly to Violet Glasspool as he helped her into her chair. 'He really is quite senile.'

'He is approaching his seventieth year,' she said in a whisper. 'It is only modern science that keeps him alive.'

'Shall we be seated?' said Bacon in a practised tone. 'What a large room they have allocated to us. As if, at any moment, the doors might burst open and the authors of all those poems before us might rush through and sit at our feet, awaiting our judgements.'

Alarmed by this unpleasant prospect, Antick stared hard at the doors. Through the smeared exteriors of the windows a sudden shaft of sun illuminated the stains on the carpet. A waiter set five plates of salmon mousse upon the table. It was thickly jellied and decorated with carved radishes. The poets sat down quickly and Bacon, the last to subside, looked curiously at the fifth place.

'Is there perhaps a fourth judge coming to join us?' he asked Gavin Jarvis.

Antick looked at the fifth plate greedily. 'They have been over generous,' he said. 'Perhaps we might divide the surplus among ourselves . . .'

'Certainly,' said Bacon, 'unless, that is . . .' His eyes fell uncertainly on the photographer who had folded up his umbrella and was coming purposefully towards the table.

'It may well be for him,' he whispered and the photographer nodded and smiled and sat down unembarrassed at the fifth place.

'Lunch for him?' said Antick reaching out jealously to guard his brimming glass.

'A splash of Muscadet?' Bacon said to the photographer.

'Not for me,' he said. 'You go ahead.'

For some moments no one spoke as they ate the mousse which was sticky and tasted of glue. After several mouthfuls the photographer laid down his fork, but the poets ate everything before them. Bacon attempted to engage them in conversation.

'Has any of you judged a poetry competition before?' he said, with an expression of polite curiosity.

'Obviously you're new to the game,' said Jarvis, 'or you'd have some idea who we are. OK, I'll fill you in. Between us, Violet, and I, and, er, Antick, have judged at least fifty of these farces. We can do them in our sleep, and probably have done. So, the answer to your question is yes. But don't worry about it.'

'I'm so sorry,' said Bacon. 'This is strange and unknown territory for me.'

'Forget it,' said Jarvis. He turned to Violet Glasspool. 'How's Alan? I thought *Return to Colonus* was a really ambitious piece of writing.'

'Your husband?' said Bacon, determined to keep up.

'He's away, on holiday. He's a little run down,' said

17

Violet Glasspool sadly, since her marriage was in a state of crisis. 'The reviews upset him.'

'Bastards,' said Jarvis savagely. 'But poets like Snapper will always be trashed by low-order, low-grade chauvinists like Walter Dove.' Jarvis ran his hand through his hair so that it stood upright in luxuriant spirals.

The waiters removed the salmon mousse and returned with a dish of grilled lamb cutlets. 'Splendid, quite splendid,' said Antick, wishing they could have run to a roast.

'Quite a good spread we give you,' said Bacon, refilling the glasses. 'But happily we can enjoy it with a clear conscience since we have met in furtherance of such a worthwhile cause.'

Jarvis sawed a piece of meat off his bone.

'Worthwhile?' he said. 'Can't we just be honest and admit that we're all taking part here in a giant public relations exercise. Every year some self-regarding capitalist mouths the same, tired platitudes about competitions like this being a good thing. For whom? For people like us, who get a free lunch. And for people like you, who get a lot of free advertising.'

'Oh Gavin, that's rather severe,' said Violet Glasspool, who gave classes in creative writing at the Thames Valley Polytechnic. 'I'm sure competitions play an important part in encouraging people to write more poetry.'

'Poetry?' said Jarvis. 'Don't let's kid ourselves that what we're doing has anything to do with poetry. We're simply celebrating the last rites of a dying culture, rewarding the perpetuators of received standards of taste with large, cash prizes.'

'Dear me,' said Bacon.

'OK, so thousands of people have forked out their four pounds to enter,' Jarvis went on. 'What does that prove? That middle-class housewives and frustrated civil servants are still able to regurgitate the weary, old clichés about spring, love, or death. Their ideas are years behind what poets are feeling now. There was no originality, no response to socio-political changes in society. No wonder the standards are so low.'

'Not a good year?' said Bacon.

'Pretty bad, I'm afraid,' said Violet.

'Fucking awful,' said Jarvis.

'Could you pass the salt, please,' said Antick, cramming bread and butter into his mouth.

'It's as if English poetry ground to a halt after Housman,' said Jarvis. 'No grasp of alternative forms – beat poetry, hunters' prayers, incantations, haikus, rants . . .'

Violet Glasspool banged the table. 'But the big themes will always recur. People will always write about the great issues of love and death – I had a lot of poems about nuclear war for example – because they touch what is deepest in the human spirit. Unfortunately people think their poems are good because they express *their* feelings. Whereas most efforts don't quite work because –'

'Because people who write poetry don't bother to read any,' Jarvis interrupted.

Bacon, one of the guilty, stared down into his wine glass.

'A lot of people think reading poetry will somehow influence them and spoil their ideas,' said Violet.

'If only it did,' said Jarvis.

Antick scraped his plate and looked up. 'I have made my short list,' he said, 'so I know which poem I am backing to win. But I thought the general standard was rather good. I had quite a few catchy numbers in my batch. One I remember about a student drama group performing in an old people's home struck me as rather good; and I had a most effective poem about a snorkeler.'

Jarvis exchanged a smile with Violet Glasspool. 'Didn't do much for me.'

Bacon decided that the poets were forming unhelpful alliances.

'We are having a great deal of pleasure,' he said, 'in

choosing a site for the presentation of the Coote & Balding Award. Our decision, I think, will be Banting, which is the home of our oldest and largest factory as well as an expanding new town.'

'It has a second-rate College of Higher Education,' said Antick pleasantly. 'I once attended an Arts Symposium there, although the hospitality was far from generous. I believe the town was once a pretty place.'

'Will the presentation be in College?' said Violet Glasspool. 'One always welcomes the chance to immerse oneself again in a student atmosphere. It makes one so nostalgic to see all those young people staying up too late and arguing so fiercely with each other.'

'No, no,' said Bacon. 'One of the larger hotels would be more appropriate. We do not want to cultivate a, shall we say, a snooty image. "Poetry for All" is our motto. We are planning a large reception.'

'Excellent idea,' said Antick. 'You would run to champagne?'

'Most certainly,' said Bacon.

'Since you're new to this racket,' said Jarvis, 'let me give you some advice. All you have to do is make sure there's a seminar afterwards to which you invite, me, Violet and –' Jarvis gestured silently towards Antick. 'The winners read out their poems; we read out some of ours. And everyone's happy.'

Jarvis laughed. Bacon, doing his job well, also laughed immoderately. He glanced at his watch and noted that there were at least two hours to go before the poets could be dispatched. He drained his glass.

The waiter brought in a pudding, livid as a bruise, which swayed and bounced, promising to discharge its pinnacled topping of whipped cream. The photographer rejected it at once and Bacon asked for cheese. Antick held out his plate.

Dipping scornfully past him, the waiter brought the pudding to Violet Glasspool depositing, as he did so, a liberal smear of the synthetic cream upon her hair. The cream hung and trembled there as she helped herself to the pudding's dark interiors.

The photographer smoked a cigarette.

Violet turned to him vivaciously. 'I suppose all this talk about poetry is very boring for you?' she said. The photographer smiled and said nothing.

'Delicious pudding,' said Antick. 'Are you sure you won't have some, Mr Bacon?'

Bacon shook his head and watched the cream in Violet's hair now firmly fixed like an elaborate decoration. She finished her pudding. The photographer leaned forward. 'Cigarette?'

'No thanks,' said Violet. 'I prefer my own.' She opened a packet of untipped Players.

'Oh please,' said Bacon, suddenly conscious of his duties as sponsor. 'Let me offer you a Coote & Balding. I absolutely insist. We would be delighted.' And he produced a large box of the company's best international length low tar.

'There are peppermints,' said Antick in delight. 'I have just found a box of strong peppermints by my plate. An excellent aid to the digestion.'

The waiters removed the pudding and Bacon suggested that they should begin the judging process. He found himself affected by an almost overwhelming desire for sleep.

'We have prepared our lists,' said Antick with an eager grin. 'You will see that the excitement begins when we put our lists together.'

'Since we're hardly an homogenous panel,' said Jarvis, 'we're unlikely to agree.'

'Most unlikely,' said Antick heartily. 'Though our discussion will be all the more stimulating for that. For myself, I should like to say that the criteria by which I have selected what I thought were the best poems, by which I mean the poems which seemed to me –'

'Cut the criteria, Howard,' said Jarvis. 'Why don't you just get on with your list?'

'Nevertheless,' said Antick, remembering again the

days of his youthful triumph, when Eliot had actually leaned forward and asked him for a cigarette, 'nevertheless I, for one, feel it is important to state the grounds on which I have attempted to judge others. I have looked, you see, for truth and originality. Truth and originality,' he repeated in ringing tones, looking defiantly round the table. 'A poet must refresh our language, he must spout like a fountain and drench us with new ways of uttering the ineffable. He must see the world more clearly than we do, he must try to express those thoughts that often lie too deep for tears . . .'

Jarvis took out his cheque book and began to fill in some empty counterfoils.

'Well, truth and originality are very important,' said Violet Glasspool, taking pity on Antick. 'But difficult perhaps to define. What I have looked for is imagination bounded by the technical limits of rhythm, rhyme, metre. Emotion, if you like, disciplined by form.'

Jarvis looked up from his cheque book. 'But Violet,' he said, 'this admirable declaration of faith simply underlines your subliminal acceptance of the rules imposed by the taste-makers of a capitalist, empiricist culture.'

'What has rhyme to do with capitalism?' said Violet Glasspool.

'Even the simplest elements of prosody have ideological connotations,' said Jarvis. 'A whole field of aesthetics has privileged the notion of rhyme, for example, in terms of order, stability, decorum. I think we should, at least, question the historical validity of our value judgements.'

Antick suddenly leaned forward.

'Thou still unravish'd bride of quietness,
    Thou foster-child of silence and slow time,
Sylvan historian . . .

What's political about that?'

Jarvis sighed loudly. 'First,' he said, with exaggerated patience, 'it happens to be an overt statement of sexual politics, demonstrating nineteenth-century attitudes

22

towards chastity which are based on a brutal and pater-
nalistic contempt for women's rights. Second, –'

'Most interesting,' said Bacon, in an attempt to prevent
himself from yawning. 'However, time does go by and we
have undertaken to finish our meeting and vacate the
room by three.'

The photographer approached the poets with his
camera and held it towards their faces at unexpected
and unsettling angles. Self-consciously Jarvis ran a hand
through his hair. 'It's an awful mess,' he murmured. 'I
really ought to give it a quick comb.'

Violet laughed spiritedly at the sight of the camera.
Her cream adornment danced and sparkled in her hair.

'This must be really boring for you,' Jarvis said to the
photographer.

'Good heavens,' said Antick faintly. 'He's shoved that
thing right up my nose.'

'Oh, come on,' said Jarvis. 'You could be covering a war
instead of listening to us.'

The photographer fired the camera at him.

'Perhaps you're into poetry yourself,' said Jarvis.

'I'm not a great reader,' said the photographer.

'Shall we press on,' said Bacon. 'I can vouch for the effi-
cacy of the peppermints.'

An hour later Bacon's box of peppermints was empty. He
glared at the sheaf of papers spreading round him on the
table, the words staring up at him like indecipherable
fragments of a foregin langugage. 'Dead Bat on a Plate,'
he read. 'Prometheus Now.' 'My Grandmother's Cactus.'

'It is certainly difficult to make progress,' he said.

'Perhaps we might have more success,' said Antick, 'if
we were fortified with something a little stronger.'

The old boy wants a whisky, thought Bacon. Well, why
not. He thought he might like one too. He called the hostile
waiter. Antick gulped his drink and looked at Violet
Glasspool's hair with its surprising decoration. He wondered why the photographer had not removed it, but he
supposed that the fellow knew his job.

'We can all agree then,' said Bacon, 'that, "Letter to an ex-Mistress" can be excluded from our short-list.' He had assumed the role of chairman and without complaint they had submitted to his authority.

'By all means,' said Antick. 'Let us strike it from the record. What about this one?' He read:

> *Would you care to see the*
> *Gazebo? You are expected, of course,*
> *But don't put your cigarette out*
> *In the water-butt; note how the*
> *Fungus is growing under your foot*
> *Everything happened as you predicted.*
> *An alternative bird sings in the*
> *Garden, now the parrot is dead.*

"An Empty Property". Rather good I thought.'

'Well, I'm going to argue for something else,' said Violet. 'This one is called, "Beans on Toast":

> *Baked beans out of their tin*
> *come to us softened like old men's gums.*
>
> *Served on a plate they attend our*
> *hushed ministrations, the sprinkling of salt.*
>
> *Here is the acolyte's spoon, instrument*
> *of haruspication. The celebrants*
>
> *honour the orange entrails; martyred*
> *toast burns exquisitely on the grill.*

I also liked "Nocturne". It had an interesting syllabic structure that strongly appealed to me.'

'What about "Wasp in a Jam Jar"?' said Antick. 'A simpler poem, perhaps, but no less worthy for that.'

'Not on my list,' said Jarvis.

'Nor on mine, I'm afraid,' said Violet. They were both ashamed for the elderly poet.

'Then I'm afraid it has to go,' said Bacon, who had become ruthless. 'What are we left with?'

'Jarvis and I have both singled out "Memoranda to Silonus",' said Violet Glasspool, 'but I have a nagging

24

worry that there is perhaps something familiar about it. I just wonder if, by any chance, I have read it before.'

The poets gazed at Bacon who was the only person in possession of the names of the competitor. 'Quite against the rules,' he said importantly, 'for me to tell you anything about the author.'

'Yes, quite,' said Violet. 'I simply had a feeling that there was something familiar there.'

'The famous woman's intuition,' said Antick heartily. 'Well, we can't let intuition pick our winner I'm afraid.'

How tedious he was, thought Violet, when he'd had a few too many. She stared at him coldly and shuffled her papers. Bacon imagined himself dying there at the table while the poets talked on, unconscious of his slack and defeated body.

'I did not enjoy "Memoranda to Silenus",' said Antick. 'You know, I rather bet it was written by a woman.'

'I liked its limpid notation,' said Jarvis, 'and its succession of daringly inventive imagery, particularly the scene where the monkey starts throwing food at the other people in the restaurant.'

'I wonder if it is a little over-written,' said Violet.

'One verse, yes,' said Jarvis, 'where the ludic element nearly overspills into facetiousness. But a lavish disquisition on bourgeois manners which develops into an articulate political statement.'

'Yes, yes,' said Antick. 'A highly allegorical poem. But "Wasp in a Jam Jar" contains a powerful message too. And what about "The Landlord"?' he went on. 'Here was a most unusual theme where a man sees his landlord day after day as he sits in the pub drinking lager, confiding his innermost thoughts to him until finally he discovers that he has fallen in love with him.'

'Entirely predictable,' said Jarvis.

'Oh, really,' said Antick. 'I must say I don't go falling in love with the landlord of my pub every day.' He laughed at some length until his laughter once more became a paroxysm of coughing.

'Is he all right?' said Jarvis.

Bacon regarded him with some anxiety. 'Would you like a drink of water?'

'Whisky,' said Antick, gasping. Slowly his face drained of colour.

'I was quite impressed with "The Dole",' said Jarvis, when Antick was quiet. 'I liked its authentic eruption of class anger combined with a brilliant sensuousness.'

He read:

'Ennithin
  ter gerra way
from t' bairnz
  half-slewed in t'
boozir,
  starin' at t' Page Three
lass wi' big knockerz
  nowt terdo,
but pick yer noaz.'

'Forceful,' said Violet. 'But my heart always rather sinks when I see a dialect poem.'

Jarvis ignored her. 'But I'm going to back "Beyond the Zebra Crossing" to win. This is a meditation on the themes of exile and the quest for self. The motorway, gathering a multiplicity of loci into a defined continuum is the mediator, if you like, of a fragmented, multi-cultural society, while the signposts, symbolic inter-stices of time and space, indicate the grim disjunction between the literally one-way capitalist executives and the observer's sense of selfhood and personal root-lessness. In some places the interlacing of politics and descriptive discourse is a little too *voulu*; but the whole is an eloquent statement of alienation, richly prodigal of daring imagery.'

'Yes, I quite liked it,' said Violet Glasspool. 'Rather intense, but a striking command of language.'

'Not one of my favourites,' said Antick. Everyone ignored him. In some despair Bacon looked at his watch. 'I think we must try to draw things to a close.'

Gavin Jarvis looked at his watch. 'Look, could we keep

26

it short,' he said. 'I'm due at the BBC in just under an hour.'

'Are you going on the television, Gavin?' said Violet Glasspool.

'A series, actually,' said Jarvis. 'They want me to put something together for them.'

'Time is no problem for me,' said Antick, looking up hopefully. 'No problem at all. There is no necessity for me to return to Epsom tonight. Indeed, I am quite prepared to undergo the inconvenience of a night in an hotel for the sake of the judging. Indeed yes. One presumes it will be, ah, at the company's expense?'

'I think there will be no need for such extreme lengths,' said Bacon firmly. 'On my short list I have the following poems: "Memoranda to Silenus", and "Beyond the Zebra Crossing". There is Miss Glasspool's poem, "Beans on Toast", and Jarvis's contender, "The Dole". There is also "An Empty Property" and "Wasp in a Jam Jar", though the last is contentious. Any more offers?'

The poets said nothing. They had no more poems to offer. Bacon saw the face of the waiter pressed up against the door, waiting for them to go. The photographer folded up his umbrella and began to pack his canvas bag.

'Cheers,' he said, waving to the poets.

'Let me give you my number,' said Jarvis. 'You can give me a ring and take some more shots if these don't work.'

In some despair Bacon said, 'Could we perhaps agree on both "Memoranda to Silenus" and "Beyond the Zebra Crossing" as our two winners?'

'I'll buy that,' said Jarvis.

'Absolutely,' said Howard Antick. 'Yes, yes, I can agree to that.'

'Miss Glasspool?'

Violet stared at them through her thick lenses. 'Yes, except for a nagging worry I still have about "Memoranda to Silenus". I simply feel a familiarity with the style. It has something in common with the work of the early Fifties.'

'Very much Howard's period,' said Jarvis.

'Fire away,' said Antick, 'though my memory cannot now be relied upon with absolute fidelity.'

Violet shrank from his whisky breath. 'It is simply that the diction – "tinnitus", "commination", "eloquent custard" – does call to mind the early work of Desmond Bysouth.'

'Bysouth? No one reads him any more, do they?' said Jarvis. 'I can't say I've ever read much of him. Howard, do you know anything about Desmond Bysouth?'

'Bysouth? Bysouth?' said Antick. 'Yes, he enjoyed a certain vogue after the war for a limited period. He is a choleric person. I don't have a great deal to do with him myself. I am not a great admirer of his work. It is always disquieting,' Antick went on, 'to reflect that even a major poet might have entered the competition anonymously, seeking, as it were, to test us. Personally nothing delights me more than when I find someone I've never heard of writing a poem of undoubted quality. But this is certainly an accomplished poem. The writer knew what he was about.'

'Anyone is allowed to enter?' said Violet Glasspool.

'According to the rules,' said Bacon, 'no one is barred. Since everything is submitted anonymously you could, in theory, be passing judgement on the most famous writers of our age.'

'Why should someone like Bysouth enter the competition?' said Jarvis.

'Of course,' said Violet, 'we don't know if it is him. It's only my hunch.'

'The question is,' said Bacon, 'do you want to make the poem a winner?'

The poets considered this.

'Had it not been suggested that this was the work of some well-known poet, that is, Desmond Bysouth,' said Antick, 'I would certainly have said yes.'

'So would I,' said Jarvis. 'We've only got Violet's word for it.'

'Well, don't blame me,' she said.

'Very well,' said Bacon, sensing the end of the struggle. 'It seems we have our two winners, ladies and gentlemen. You have chosen, after what has been a most lively and interesting discussion, to award the prize to "Memoranda to Silenus" and "Beyond the Zebra Crossing". Congratulations one and all.'

'Fair enough, fair enough,' said Antick. 'Yes, that's a very fair choice.'

'Well,' said Jarvis, 'that's it. Let's hope the punters are satisfied.'

'I have an idea,' said Antick, consulting his watch, 'that the sun must be over the yard arm. Yes, they're open.'

Bacon stood up. His moment of release was at hand.

'Such a stimulating way of passing the afternoon,' said Antick rising unsteadily. 'It reminds me of the days when I used to come home every day after nine exhausting hours reading publishers' proofs to a mountain of manuscripts like the ones we have dealt with today, all sent in from people begging me to publish their poems in my magazine.'

'Time to move,' said Jarvis.

'Of course, in those days I could read over a hundred poems in an afternoon. Most were bad, yes, but whether I published them or not, I would always write to their authors, explaining why I had reached my decision. It was exhausting work, but I like to think that they derived some benefit, some therapy, perhaps, from the enterprise. And I might claim some credit for discovering some of today's leading writers. It was about thirty years ago, I suppose, when I first published Robert Bantam. It gave him tremendous encouragement. So much so, indeed, that he paid me the honour of a visit. I can remember quite clearly the tremendous shock I had when I saw him coming up the drive to my house in Epsom.'

'Really?' said Bacon politely, hovering at the table.

'Yes,' said Antick. 'This fellow came up the path,

stuck out his hand and said, "Mr Antick, this is a great privilege." I said, "Why it is Robert Bantam" – he was, you see, not at all well known in those days – "won't you come in and have some tea?" And he said, "Well, as a matter of fact I came to ask you to lend me ten pounds." "Ten pounds?" I said. I can tell you that in those days it was a considerable sum of money, much more than it is worth these days unfortunately. However, I looked at him and said, "Ten pounds?" "Only until Tuesday," he said, "I find myself rather short." "Well," I said, "let me give you some tea first and then we can talk about this ten pounds." So he came inside and ate a great many of my late wife's home-made biscuits.'

'Did you give him the money?' said Jarvis, wondering with interest if Antick made a habit of subsidising younger poets.

'I did not,' Antick said with dignity. 'It was a large sum and I did not have it in the house. Besides, I could not afford to do so. After his tea, Bantam did not leave for some hours and drank a large amount of whisky.'

Gavin Jarvis stepped elegantly past Bacon as he made for the door. 'It's been great fun,' he said. 'See you at Banting.'

'Oh, Gavin,' said Violet Glasspool, 'if you're going to the BBC I wonder if I could possibly scrounge a lift. It's minutes from my flat.'

'Sorry, Violet,' said Jarvis, picking up his crash helmet, 'but I'm meeting someone first.'

'Oh, forgive me,' said Violet, gathering up her papers in some confusion.

'Thank you so much,' said Bacon, 'for all the good work. Coote & Balding is most grateful to you. Thank you so much for coming.' Earnestly he hoped that Violet Glasspool would not ask him to stay for a drink with her.

'Violet, my dear,' said Antick, 'what about a cocktail to set you on your way?'

'No thank you, Howard, dear,' she said, pulling a head scarf over the cream on her hair. 'Oh dear, there's something sticky up here,' she said in some distress, examining her white, smeared fingers. 'Howard, there is something in my hair.' Antick was circling the table collecting up the remainder of the peppermints. Discountenanced, Violet looked up at the ceiling, wondering if the strange substance had perhaps dropped from its dusty heights.

Antick strolled over to Bacon. 'A quick one?'

'Thank you, no. I have to catch my train.'

'Splendid,' said Antick.

'You have a train?'

'Yes, yes I do. But I'm just wondering whether to make a night of it.'

'Alas, you will excuse me if I say goodbye?'

'Yes,' said Antick. 'There is just the matter of the expenses.'

'Expenses?' said Bacon.

'Ten pounds would do nicely,' said Antick, 'for the train fare.' Bacon produced a ten pounds from his wallet.

'Much obliged,' said Antick, walking unsurely from the Rembrandt Room bent on livelier entertainment.

When all the poets had gone, Bacon consulted his list which disclosed the identity of the competitors. The name of Desmond Bysouth was nowhere to be seen. Well, he thought, it was nothing for him to worry about. Nothing to do with him. And he went out into the crisp evening bound for the clearer air of Surrey.

2

Poets, eloquent and contentious, bickering and vicious
raced through Bacon's dreams that night. His bedtime
Ovaltine could not quieten the anxious revolutions of his
brain as he lay arguing with bloated, furious old men
who harangued him in hotel bars and read unintelligible
extracts from their own works. Waking suddenly at
three, Bacon saw by his side the slackened shape of his
wife, Doreen, and he was reassured by her bulk, a territory forbidden to poetry and song. As the constellations
wheeled overhead she slept rhythmically, her mouth
slightly open, her brain occupied by slight, perplexing
dreams. Beyond the fastness of their bedroom, Bacon
knew, were other sleepers, breathing quietly into the
prosperous night, people like Bacon, exhausted by pro-
ductive work, enriched quite justly by its rewards.
Bankers, company chairmen, the captains of industry
slept there in the Surrey calm, renewing their energies
for the struggle next day.

On bedside tables their reading matter was strewn,
discarded by a limp hand as sleep overcame it. As their
minds prepared for sleep, these great men were soothed
with words, opiate phrases, narcotic paragraphs which
lulled them into stupor. What did they choose to send
them insensible into the night? Some passage from the
classics, a draught of Shakespeare, Milton or Plato?
Or words wrung out by young men during the small
anguished hours before dawn, words such as Desmond
Bysouth or, in his younger days, Howard Antick might
have set down with tears in their eyes?

Unfortunately, throughout the private Surrey lanes there was none that had turned to poetry. At their bedsides were magazines containing articles on gardening, or cookery recipes, and the conveniently sized pamphlets of the *Reader's Digest*. Exhausted by the labours of the day they craved the potency of easily understood and undemanding sentiments:

Life is like painting a picture,
* not doing an addition sum.*

Stretching out his hand, Bacon encountered a booklet telling him how to remove household stains. Soothed and reassured by the discovery that the application of a hydrogen peroxide solution will quickly remove tea stains from a blanket, he drifted into a light sleep as the first signs of the approaching day turned the eastern sky a lighter purple. Out over the North Sea, over the Channel which Bacon crossed every summer, the dawn spread, advancing over London, over Surrey and over Slough where the grudging commuters were stirring, reluctant to acknowledge the arrival of a new day.

Eddie Rosemary had risen early, long before his neighbours had drawn their curtains to admit the light. From his kitchen the electric light was like a beacon in the darkness, but he was not at home. Some ten minutes' walking distance from Appletree Crescent, he was standing in a field where thistles and coarse rushes were beaded with moisture from the dew. Rosemary walked carefully in rubber boots down the sloping field and climbed over a barbed wire fence. Behind him a screen of trees covered the summit of a hill. As he advanced through the second field, there was an area of marsh where a concrete tunnel was whitely luminous in the dark. If Rosemary looked to the east he could see the meadows stretching towards the boundaries of a council estate. If he turned towards the tunnel he saw the broad sweep of the motorway as it cut a triumphant path through the Berkshire countryside. Through the tunnel, twice a day, incurious cows were driven to be milked while a hasty succession of cars passed loudly above their heads.

With concentration Rosemary enumerated the features of the countryside. His feet sank through the spongy grass into water as he took out his notebook. Thistles, he observed. Cowpats, and, in the distance, cows. The unremarkable rural commonplaces. He noted a discarded tin can, once containing lemonade. In the thistles there was a small piece of torn, blue plastic. Dissatisfied with his observations Rosemary went further down the field.

The first cars of the morning were already roaring above him as Rosemary stared without pleasure at the natural coverings of the earth. Although he believed himself to be quite without sensibility to scenic beauty, he diligently recorded visual changes in the landscape day by day as a technical exercise. Rosemary looked at the lightening sky and tried to think of adjectives to describe the precise nature, size and shape of the clouds. Throwing back his head he breathed the exhaust fumes of the traffic. *Viscous, drifting,* he wrote, *fleeced, flecked, flocked.* Rosemary tried to think about the sky but the noise of the cars was now impossible to ignore, a series of low whining vibrations that pulsed through his head. He turned his attention to the cars and watched the shining forms as they glittered against the grey sky. They were of absorbing interest. And the men inside them? How could he draw it all together? He looked at his watch and reflected that he must not be late for work. He turned away from the tunnel and felt hungry. Although he wore an anorak and trousers over his pyjamas, Rosemary was cold. *Raw condensation,* he wrote in his notebook, holding it before him for a studied moment. For several minutes he stood motionless there in the field, self-conscious and delighting in his singularity, so that if any of the drivers in the speeding cars should glance down in their rapid passage at seventy or eighty miles an hour, they would see in the fields below them an

35

astonishing thing, a man composing poetry.

But the cars passed by and their drivers saw nothing but the road, their minds absorbed by the weather forecast and the negotiations that lay ahead of them. Breathless and dizzy with his exalted vision of himself, Rosemary stood for another precious minute, then turned back through the fields to the road which led to his own housing development, remote from the quotidian affairs which preoccupied his neighbours. He walked noisily down his front path, waving his arms and hoping for comment and suspicion from the housewives who were now busy in their kitchens. But no one twitched their curtains aside; no one observed his eccentricity. Rosemary entered his house unremarked.

Deciding he had no time for breakfast, he ran to the station eating a Mars bar. In any case, his sparsely furnished kitchen would have yielded nothing, since it contained only several pints of milk which had been resting in his refrigerator for the last three weeks. A slight odour clung to him as he walked rapidly down the ramp to the station platform. Discovering he had no clean shirts he had been compelled to recover one from his strong-smelling laundry basket. His notebook, transferred from his anorak pocket, was unused during the journey to Cartons (UK) Ltd where he worked in the accounts department. He found nothing to write about on the crowded train.

'Good morning,' said Bacon, stepping through the heavy glass doors which led to the interior of Coote & Balding House.

'Good morning, Mr Bacon,' said the receptionist, a girl chosen for her golden ripeness and air of expertise.

'Rather cold this morning.'

'Chilly.'

'Yes, there is an autumnal air to the day. Season of mists and mellow fruitfulness, as the poet said.'

Bacon stepped softly over the golden carpet and rose in the silent lift to his own second-floor office, appropriately remote from the chairman, who occupied the sixth floor. 'Poetry competition,' his diary reminded him. The unfamiliar excitement caused him to smile quietly to himself. He opened his briefcase and took out the competition papers. Here were the now familiar winning poems, written by Eddie Rosemary and someone called J. W. Blanks. Bacon picked up the telephone.

Inside Rosemary's austere house the telephone rang unanswered.

Inside a telephone box at Waterloo Station the telephone rang and rang.

Bacon put down the receiver. 'No reply,' he said, deflated, his moment of power postponed. 'No one at either number. Dear me, how annoying.'

His secretary brought him coffee, cream and sugar arranged on a silver tray.

'Thank you, Cheryl,' said Bacon automatically.

Cheryl, a girl slightly less golden than the receptionist, smiled and revealed sharp, pointed teeth.

'I'll try again,' said Bacon. 'They might have just popped out for a paper.'

Inside the empty house the telephone shrilled again.

Inside the telephone box at Waterloo Station the telephone rang and rang.

Throughout the day Bacon made unsuccessful attempts to contact the competition winners. Eventually he sent them both a telegram. *Congratulations*, he wrote. *You have won the Coote & Balding Poetry Competition. Please ring Hubert Bacon (Organiser) at once.* Cheryl brought him afternoon tea with assorted biscuits.

'Nothing more we can do today, Cheryl,' said Bacon. 'Could you book me in to see the chairman some time this week? I need to know his thoughts about the presentation.'

Rosemary walked slowly down Appletree Crescent towards his empty house. His alone was dark. Everywhere lights blazed at his neighbours' windows as the housewives prepared supper for their husbands in steamy kitchens. Exhausted by his repetitive work in the accounts department Rosemary rubbed his red, strained eyes. The house, cold and silent, received him. Rosemary walked through the darkness into his sitting room where he switched on the harsh overhead light. The room was bare except for a three-piece suite in green velvet, a bookcase and a television set. Rosemary laid down his briefcase and turned on the television where a concerned young woman told him of the hardships experienced by homeless families in the Slough area, victims of an uncaring social security system. He walked uneasily round the room and then went to the kitchen to pour himself a drink. As he went back past the front door he noticed that there was an envelope lying on the doormat. It was blue and orange; Rosemary's heart leaped. Carefully, as though it contained explosive, he picked it up and laid it on the kitchen table. He poured himself a whisky. After some moments he opened the envelope and his hands began to shake so much that some of the whisky was spilled. Rosemary hastily drained the glass. His lips parted and he gasped through his open mouth like an athlete exhausted by a sprint.

He ran out of the kitchen. He ran upstairs then down again and round the sitting room. He jumped towards the ceiling, touching it with the outstretched tips of his fingers. He lay on the floor and drummed his heels on the carpet. He waved his arms and danced wildly on the spot. The silent house stood amazed. Rosemary poured another whisky. Tears welled in his eyes and ran unchecked down his cheeks. He sat in his green velvet chair, gripped its arms and wept.

The television spoke on. Families were living on less than £20 a week, old people were dying of cold. After some minutes Rosemary went over to the set and switched it off. Then he knelt in front of the screen and looked carefully at a photograph on top of the set.

It was a picture of a child, a boy running across a field in the middle of summer. There was sunshine behind the boy and this blazed around him, lighting up his face, burning at his head like a halo. Caught at that particular moment, lit by the sunlight, the boy stared into the camera, his eyes shining with joy as though he was rejoicing in a secret he would never share with the onlooker. Rosemary silently considered the picture of his own incorruptible youth, trying to recognise the boy he had once been, whose perceptions he had now forgotten. His hands shook and he gazed into the shining face with wonder.

3

'Look your best,' wrote Nina Cleverly, 'by velvet night or tweedy day.' Her attention wandered. She made adjustments to the shape of her fingernails.

The office was warm, almost suffocating. From behind pots of green, trailing-leaved plants, women stared at each other or talked with animation into telephones. Under the fluorescent light their faces were strained and yellowish. The office was open plan, divided only by partitions and as the visitor wandered through the maze of screens he was assailed by the clash of scents which permeated the air, generated by the various occupants of the editorial floor.

'Nina!'

Nina Cleverly heard the voice of the editor ring out down the long, carpeted corridor. Guiltily she sprang up and almost ran into Madge Driller's office. Here the air was so thick with *Fantôme de l'Opéra* that it was almost impossible to breathe.

Madge Driller, editor of *Sparkle!* magazine, sat behind her desk and took up a paper knife. One of her secretaries brought her a glass and an effervescent tablet of Vitamin C. Madge Driller lifted the carafe of water on her desk and silently filled the glass. She dropped the tablet into the water where it turned orange and began to fizz.

'We have decided,' she said, 'that *Sparkle!* needs more arts coverage.'

Nina Cleverly nodded pliantly. The paper knife was pointing directly towards her.

'Our most recent readership profile suggests that *Sparkle!* readers are buying more books, not just romantic fiction but real books, biographies, history and –' Madge Driller hesitated, '– poetry. We need to reflect this trend in our magazine,' she said, draining her glass of Vitamin C. Its rim was smeared by the vivid red imprint of her lips. 'I want us to be the thinking woman's magazine. I want us to be better, smarter, brighter . . .'

Nina Cleverly nodded uneasily.

A rack of dresses was wheeled into the editor's office. Madge Driller considered a white dress which one of the fashion editors held out before her. 'Yes,' she said slowly. 'Yes, I like it, but I don't understand . . . what it's trying to say.'

The fashion editor retreated wheeling the dresses before her.

Madge Driller lit a cigarette. 'Now,' she said, 'there's a feeling that poetry is becoming an exciting scene. I want us to explore it. Get the feeling of poetry in London. Who are the poets? Where are they? Do they still starve in garrets? Are we all poets? *Sparkle!* will run its own competition. The winner gets a free weekend for two in Paris plus a week's creative writing tuition course with a famous poet. And the runners-up will go in a coach party to the presentation of the Coote & Balding prize at Banting. I want some interviews.'

'Certainly,' said Nina Cleverly.

'Remember, I want an intellectual piece. Talk about poetry, get the feel of it. Interview the Coote & Balding winners. Make poetry accessible. Working girls can be poets too. Explore the importance of poetry womanwise; you know, poetry is like hang-gliding – daunting at first but absolutely breathtaking once you get the feel of it. Walter Dove, who's a first-rate critic, and editor of *Advance*, will give you all the background. He's a dear friend of mine. Are you interested in poetry yourself?'

'Well –' said Nina Cleverly.

'That's great,' said Madge Driller. 'Set to work.'

Nina Cleverly left the room and rang up Walter Dove at *Advance*.

'Dove speaking,' he said.

'Good morning,' said Nina Cleverly. 'I've rung to ask your thoughts about poetry.'

'Good morning,' said Hubert Bacon. 'A rather damp morning today, I fear.'

The golden receptionist nodded sympathetically.

'The train was most unpleasantly crowded,' said Bacon. 'They are running late because of leaves on the track. One needs one's coffee.'

The receptionist smiled again in a superior way. She did not make coffee for anyone, indeed at eleven she had her own tray brought to her by Bacon's secretary.

While Cheryl was bringing him his tea, he noticed that his telegram to J. W. Blanks had been returned by the Post Office. The telephone rang. 'Hello?' said Bacon.

'Hello?' said Eddie Rosemary.

'This is Hubert Bacon,' said Bacon. 'To whom am I speaking?'

'It is Eddie Rosemary,' said Rosemary nervously 'I have received a telegram from you. It is Eddie Rosemary speaking.'

Unprepared for his message of congratulations, Bacon nevertheless embarked on a short speech.

'I am most grateful to you,' said Rosemary. 'I didn't dare to hope . . .'

'Well done,' said Bacon. 'I will be sending you details of our presentation ceremony, but in the meanwhile may I give you the exciting news that you are to be featured in *Sparkle!*'

'What is *Sparkle!?*'

'A magazine,' said Bacon. 'A woman's magazine, though I must confess I'm not a reader myself. It's giving in-depth coverage of our competition.'

'I think I'd rather not –'

'There's no need for any anxiety,' said Bacon smoothly. 'I don't think they will need to dig too deeply, you know. Just a short interview would be in order.'

There was a short pause.

43

'Well, many congratulations,' said Bacon. 'Our cheque will be presented at the ceremony, and no doubt it will be a welcome benefit to you, or so we hope.'

'Yes, thank you. I – I'm most grateful,' said Rosemary.

'Then I look forward to our meeting in Banting,' said Bacon. 'Very well done. A marvellous achievement.'

The telephone rang again.

'Hello,' said Bacon. 'Bacon speaking.'

'This is the operator,' a woman said. 'I understand you have been making enquiries regarding an unobtainable number.'

'Yes, I can't get through at all. Frankly, is this what we pay our telephone bills for?'

The operator's voice hardened. 'The number you are trying is that of a public telephone box at Waterloo Station. Please note that we do not encourage subscribers to ring the boxes.'

'I was not attempting to ring the box,' said Bacon in indignation. 'I was under the impression that I was contacting a private person.'

'The box is out of order.'

'That's of no interest to me,' said Bacon, and replaced the receiver. A sense of apprehension seized him as he realised that all was not as it should be. A public telephone box at Waterloo? Perhaps there had been a misprint on the list?

The telephone rang again.

'Hello,' said Bacon. 'This is Hubert Bacon.'

'Hello, hello,' said Violet Glasspool. 'I'm sorry to say that I'm the harbinger of doom.' Her voice sounded strangely slurred.

'Miss Glasspool?' said Hubert Bacon. 'How are you? What can I do for you?'

'Not too good,' said Violet. 'Look, I've made a terrible discovery.'

'Terrible? But what has happened. Not bad news, I hope.'

'The worst possible news. I blame myself entirely.'

'Surely not.'

'Yes, I insist on taking full responsibility.'

'Is there anything I can do to help?'

'You must go to the Banjo Club and tell him the truth. I told them the poem was familiar and indeed it is.'

'The poem?' said Bacon. 'The poem by J. W. Blanks?'

'So-called,' said Violet, and laughed unsteadily.

'I'm sorry to have to tell you that we've been unable to contact Mr Blanks. A telegram sent to his address has been returned by the Post Office and his telephone number turns out to be that of a telephone box at Waterloo Station.

'The poem was written by Desmond Bysouth,' said Violet Glasspool. 'I looked it up. You can imagine my horror when I came across "Memoranda to Silenus" in Bysouth's first collection of poems, *Bulletin from Narcissus*. I happen to possess a copy, although few people have ever read it. I turned over the pages, hoping I had made a mistake, but there was no doubt at all. The book sold only twenty copies. It is almost a collector's item now. I blame myself – if only I had insisted. But you were all so certain I was wrong.'

'This is grave news,' said Bacon. 'Grave and distressing news. There's no chance that you're mistaken?'

Violet Glasspool laughed. 'I'm still young,' she said. 'My whole life is before me.'

'I'm so sorry,' said Bacon. 'Dear me, the line is very bad.'

Violet Glasspool was twenty years old when she first met Desmond Bysouth at a party given by a fellow Girtonian who had entered the world of advertising. Bysouth wore a large black hat and was employed to write advertising slogans persuading people to eat more fruit. He had a bright red face made unsightly by pimples. Violet remembered his fondness for whisky. It had been a whirlwind romance, she told herself, a heady thing of the moment. Bysouth had disappeared for a considerable time after their marriage and reappeared with no explanation as to where he had been. Violet had composed poems and submitted them to him for approval or criticism and sometimes he would pronounce like an oracle on their worth, while she sat at his feet pouring him whisky. More frequently, however, Bysouth did not bother to read them at all and they would have fierce, explosive arguments that brought cries of complaint from their neighbours and tears of recrimination and remorse from them both.

'He swept me off my feet,' Violet said incoherently. 'I was only a girl, a mere child . . .'

'Miss Glasspool? Is everything all right?'

'If only I had insisted,' said Violet. 'I feel my whole reputation to be undermined. You will find him at the Banjo Club.'

'Bysouth?'

'I'm afraid that I must go,' said Violet.

'One moment please, Miss Glasspool.'

'I'm rather unwell. Goodbye.'

Bacon telephoned Howard Antick.

'Antick here,' said the elderly poet.

'How do you do. Hubert Bacon here.'

'Who is that?'

'Bacon. I'm the man from Coote & Balding.'

'Ah yes, of course,' said Antick. 'I'm afraid I must ask you to speak up. I'm not terribly *au fait* with the telephone.'

'Can you tell me anything,' said Bacon, enunciating clearly, 'about a poet called Desmond Bysouth?'

'Who?' said Antick.

'Bysouth!' said Bacon, shouting into the mouthpiece. They conducted the rest of the conversation at shouting level.

'Is he still alive?' said Antick.

'I believe so. I gather he's a contemporary of yours.'

'He enjoyed a vogue after the Second World War for a limited period, do you see? He was a choleric person. I did not have a great deal to do with him myself. I am not, as it happens, a great admirer of his work.'

'I see.'

'What?'

'I am most grateful to you.'

46

'I do not believe that many people read him today,' said Antick, 'although perhaps the younger poets may have, ah, rediscovered him. As I remember he was often inclined to violence. You should ask Violet Glasspool all about him. She was once Mrs Bysouth but she keeps very quiet about that these days.'

'Mrs Bysouth? You mean they were married?'

'They were man and wife for a short time. I believe they were not suited for each other.'

In some surprise Bacon considered the unfortunate news. They had, it seemed, been duped by a hoaxer who called himself J. W. Blanks who had stolen the work of a published poet for money. Bacon's spirits sank. The announcement of the competition winners had appeared in all the papers, accompanied by a rather blurred picture of the judges reaching their decision. It did none of them justice, Bacon thought, especially Violet Glasspool with her strangely decorated hair. It was unthinkable that they should publish a correction. The Coote & Balding chairman would not agree to that idea at all. Bacon's telephone rang again.

'Hello, hello?' Antick shouted.

'Bacon speaking.'

'Bacon?'

'Yes.'

'I say,' said Antick, 'if you're going around chasing up Bysouth – if he's still alive – you won't say that you've talked to me will you? He's a fearfully unpleasant sort of chap and he would stop at nothing –' his voice cracked with nervousness '– to get his own back. You don't mind my asking?'

'Not at all.'

'Thank you so much,' said Antick.

After a short and unpleasant interview with the chairman, Bacon left his office just before lunch, armed with the necessary street directions for finding the Banjo Club. An interview with Bysouth, however unattractive the prospect, was necessary to make sure he would not put in an official complaint.

'If the press get hold of this,' Bacon told himself, 'it will be dynamite.' Thrilled with the important secret he set off through the streets of Mayfair with fear and a strange exhilaration in his heart.

4

'How long have you been a journalist?' asked Walter Dove, smiling at Nina Cleverly. They were sitting in his small office at *Advance*, surrounded by piles of books which seemed likely at any moment to fall from their precarious heights. They were all review copies, sent free by publishers hoping for a notice and later sold at some profit by Dove who had established generous terms with a second-hand bookshop. Old, yellowing proofs spilled over his desk and there was a mustiness in the room as if the outer air had not penetrated it for many years. Indeed, from Dove's seclusion it was hard to realise that a world existed outside his windows, which were grimy and caked with mud and accretions of dirt thrown up off the busy street.

'It surely can't have been more than a few months,' he went on, breathing rather heavily through his nose. 'You can't be more than twenty, or do all you young girls look like that these days?'

Dove tipped back his head and laughed in a whinnying gust through lips that remained permanently moist. His grey hair was curiously cut a uniform length all over his head so that it flopped over his forehead.

'I'm older than you suppose,' said Nina Cleverly. 'I've been writing for *Sparkle!* for two years.'

'Two years,' said Dove, affecting surprise. 'You know, Madge Driller is one of my greatest friends. A remarkable, fascinating woman. She is brusque, yes, hard, up to a point, but only with a sort of diamond brilliance. A first-rate editor, Nina, and you'll learn a lot from her.'

'I'm sure you're right,' said Nina Cleverly. 'She suggested that you would be able to give me some background material.'

'Yes, background,' said Dove thoughtfully. 'Would you like some tea?'

'Thank you.'

'Doris,' Dove said, calling his secretary. 'A cup of tea please, and we'd like a nice biccy if you can find one.'

Dove's secretary promptly appeared with a tray.

'Now,' said Dove, 'chocolate or plain? You look like a very clever girl, Nina. I'd love to read some of the articles you've written.'

'I'm sure you wouldn't find them interesting.'

Dove rolled his eyes in disbelief.

'They're all about how to lose ten pounds in a week or wear a dress that will change your life.'

'Women always want to change their lives,' said Dove. 'That's one of the most predictable things about them. But I'm sure it's valuable training for you, Nina. Life is all before you; the world's your oyster, the sky's your limit.'

'I expect so,' said Nina Cleverly.

Bacon stepped confidently across Berkeley Square towards the neon-illuminated sign of the Ritz. He strode down Piccadilly, past expensive shops, airline offices and a sports outfitters where a stuffed fox dressed in a hunting jacket and grasping a whip in its paw stared out at him. At Piccadilly Circus he was nearly knocked down and killed by a bus which approached him rapidly as he stepped out to cross the road. Uneasily Bacon continued his journey and after several minutes lost his way in the maze of shops and restaurants behind Shaftesbury Avenue.

Unsettling sights now began to disturb him. From all sides, it seemed, the bodies of women displayed themselves for him. Wherever he turned his eyes, trying to avoid the menacing sights, he gazed upon another naked breast spilling from a black corset, another thigh bulging over a tight stocking top. Black rectangles obscured certain parts of bodies like obscene postage stamps. He could not escape them. Lights flashed, and music, cheap and reverberating, assaulted his ears. He turned down a side street in confusion and found himself confronted by a dark-skinned man standing outside a fluttering plastic curtain.

'Come inside, sir?' the man said. 'Lovely girls.'

'No,' said Bacon, hurrying past.

'Lovely girls,' the man said, 'all sixteen, very young, very pretty.'

Bacon almost ran down the street. He had had no idea of the vice, the unspeakable vice that was taking place minutes from the office. He had been faithful to his wife for more than thirty years. A vision of Cheryl, corseted and crammed into tight stockings suddenly rose in his mind. Appalled, he thrust the image away. The vision returned, with some persistence. Bacon felt himself excited and ashamed. He shut his eyes, then opened them and stared into the windows of a newsagent's shop, hoping to recall the real, respectable world of the newspaper headlines. But behind the glass he saw more women, displaying parts of themselves, staring at him, unashamed and inviting. He passed another man who smiled and nodded at him under the red neon sign, which said 'Spanking Cinema'. Bacon was deeply troubled. He thought once again of Cheryl; this time she leaned towards him and parts of her body swung towards him, released from their scanty black underwear. Bacon reached to grasp them. Gasping, he stopped and leaned against a lamp post. He was sweating and the collar of his shirt was tight. He thought about his wife, Doreen, but Cheryl reached towards him and began to remove her stockings. Bacon turned round and went back to the Spanking Cinema.

'Striptease, lovely girls, live,' the man said.

Bacon plunged through the plastic curtain and held out ten pounds with a shaking hand. The smell of cheap scent

51

rose to meet him as he almost ran down the narrow stairs leading to wine-red darkness and oblivion.

'Tell me,' said Walter Dove. 'What do you think of this Medoc? I think it's awfully good for the price. Unassuming, but very drinkable.'

'Delicious,' said Nina Cleverly. They were sitting in a crowded wine bar, squashed close together on adjacent stools. Dove's breath was hot and tainted as he leaned forward and said, 'Tell me, Nina, do you like going to see films in the evening?'

'I have to concentrate on poetry. For my article.'

'Yes, your article. I must say I admire your application. Clearly you're a very special sort of writer, Nina. I think that's marvellous.'

'I have to write about the poetry scene.'

'The poetry scene? Would you like me to take you to the Terpsichore Club tonight? A. N. W. S. Savory is giving a lecture, but you might find it rather dull.'

'Will many poets be there?'

'Hundreds.'

'I see.'

'I could introduce you to some interesting people. Look,' said Dove, 'see if you can make it. Although I suppose you're going out with your boyfriend, aren't you, Nina. Why should you want to spend an evening with a dry old stick like me?'

'No, I –'

'Have you finished your beef?' said Dove assiduously. 'Then I'll just nip across to the counter and get us some Stilton. It's absolutely delicious here.'

Some time later Bacon climbed dizzily up the stairs of the Spanking Cinema. Blinded by the daylight, he blinked in confusion as he made his way towards the fluttering curtain. A group of men were sitting in the entrance, drinking tea and playing cards. In his hurry to escape, Bacon struck his foot hard on something and almost fell over one of the card-player's legs. He turned to gasp an apology. An old man in a vivid flowered shirt smiled at him. 'It's all right, dear,' he said, pulling his leg, which was made of wood, closer under the table. The man waved invitingly at him. In horror Bacon ran out of the cinema, pushing his way down the crowded street. When he stopped running he realised he was quite lost.

On the corner of the street he saw a pub called the Dancing Cockerel and tremulously pushed open the door. The bar was almost empty since it was nearly closing time. A middle-aged, prematurely grey-haired man was drinking vodka at the bar, surrounded by a group of silent, unsmiling companions.

'Forgive me,' said Bacon, still shaken from his recent experiences, 'I wonder if you could kindly direct me to the Banjo Club. I believe it is somewhere in the vicinity.'

'Where?' said the grey-haired man.

'The Banjo Club,' said Bacon. 'I believe it is near here.'

From behind the bar someone emerged with a plate of fish and chips which was reverently placed before the grey-haired man. Ignoring Bacon he took up his knife and fork and began to eat, randomly putting chips in his mouth, some of which fell out again.

'Can I take it you don't know where it is?' said Bacon politely.

'You can take whatever you fucking like,' said the man, who was now trying to lodge a piece of fish on the end of his fork. 'Now fuck off. I want to eat my lunch.'

Uncertainly Bacon retreated. One of the silent drinkers looked over his shoulder. 'It's number thirty-four up the road. Turn right as you leave.'

'Thank you so much,' said Bacon. Hurriedly he left the pub as the vodka drinker slipped from his bar stool on to the floor. Almost weeping, Bacon fled from the sordid scene. And yet, was he any the less sordid himself? Wasn't he, now, one of these seedy ones, wasting their lives in a state of degradation? He felt tainted by the run-down, shabby buildings. Perhaps he might feel better after a drink.

There was a hint of rain in the air as Bacon knocked cautiously on the door of the Banjo Club.

'Good afternoon,' a fat woman said. 'Are you a member?'

'No,' said Bacon. 'I have come here to meet Mr Desmond Bysouth.'

'Just a minute. You're not the Old Bill?'

'Old Bill?'

'Or from the income tax?'

'No indeed,' said Bacon. 'I am a representative of the tobacco company, Coote & Balding. I have come to discuss poetry with Mr Desmond Bysouth.'

'He's over by the bar,' said the fat woman. 'Gent with ginger hair.'

Bacon stepped into the whisky-scented gloom. In the dark recesses of the club he could see dim alcoves, protected from the onlookers' curious gaze by high, curtained screens. There were a surprising number of people in the club, although it was difficult to see their faces distinctly.

'Mr Bysouth?' said Bacon unhappily, advancing towards the red-headed man.

Bysouth made no reply but stared at him, rapidly raising and lowering his sandy eyebrows.

'Mr Desmond Bysouth?'

The poet scrutinised him fiercely. Then he said: 'It is Bysouth who speaks.'

'My name is Bacon.'

Bysouth giggled.

'Hubert Bacon. I am the administrator of the Coote & Balding poetry competition. It is important that I discuss certain events with you and I was advised to contact you here at the Banjo Club. I understand that you do not have a telephone, hence my rather impromptu appearance. My apologies for disturbing your afternoon.'

Bysouth smiled, exposing terribly blackened teeth, and said, 'Would you care to buy me a drink?'

'Certainly,' said Bacon, encouraged. 'What is it to be?'

'Double whisky,' said Bysouth.

'I'll join you myself,' said Bacon, ordering drinks at the bar. What a pathetic way for a famous poet to end his days, he thought, as he handed over the whisky. So much for the life of art and letters. Poor fellow, spending his afternoons like this, wearing such horrible old clothes and really rather far from clean.

Bysouth drank the whisky with surprising speed and then said, 'Can you lend me a fiver?'

Bacon thought that he could always claim the money back on expenses. He handed over the note. Bysouth immediately went to the bar and bought two more whiskies with it.

'Cheers,' he said loudly, grinning at Bacon and once again revealing his distressing teeth.

'Cheers.'

There was a short pause.

'You may be wondering,' said Bacon, 'why I've come to see you. In fact I must discuss certain matters about the Coote & Balding poetry competition.'

'Shall I tell you what the tragedy of English poetry is?' said Bysouth loudly.

'Certainly. I should be most interested to know.'

Bysouth cleared his throat. 'The tragedy of English poetry,' he said, 'is that there's no one living in England now who would undress in public if the moment were suitable. There's no one who would work for three years on an arrangement of words and smile in the darkness. There is no one who would appear on television in a dirty collar.'

'Most interesting,' said Bacon politely.

'There are no poets in all the world,' said Bysouth, 'and the ravens mourn on the tree tops.'

'Oh come now,' said Bacon, 'there are at least two, who have won our competition.' Then he remembered the difficulties about J. W. Blanks and his optimism evaporated.

'There is a man at Oxford,' said Bysouth, 'who is paid nearly three thousand pounds to be a Professor of Poetry. He sits in the tea-shop and the undergraduates come and ask him about his life. In an age when we applaud the Professor of Poetry do we deserve to have any poets?'

'I'm not much of an expert in that field, myself,' said Bacon. 'I'm afraid I'm not a university man, although I've always argued that I learned more in the University of Life than I could have picked up from studying books.'

Bysouth ignored him. 'What does the Professor do? What does he say to the young men? What does he tell his masters, the politicians? Politicians should have nothing to do with poets, for they spread misery and lack conviction. And what does the Professor of Poetry tell them? What does he say?'

'I cannot imagine.'

'He says nothing,' said Bysouth, his voice rising. 'He is an empty vessel. Perhaps he was a poet once, but he has grown fat. Shed no tears for him since he is rich and bloated. And no one in all the world cares whether he speaks or is silent.'

Bysouth was silent for some minutes, staring into his drink.

'Well,' said Bacon, as the whisky hit his empty stomach with pleasing warmth, 'what an extraordinary world it is! Yes, this is quite an insight into Bohemian life.' His hidden sense of shame lifted a little and he laughed to himself. What would the office make of this drinking club? What would Doreen think? Dear me, thought Bacon, this really is a glimpse of the underworld, and poor old Bysouth shouting away like a madman.

He turned to the poet again. 'The reason for my visiting you,' he said carefully, 'is that there has been a rather unfortunate muddle over the poetry competition. Yes, I'm sorry to have to tell you that we cannot simply announce our winners and congratulate them, and perhaps ourselves. I'm afraid that some anonymous and unscrupulous person has submitted one of your early poems under a false name. I can only tell you how sorry we are that this has happened.'

'Which poem?'

' "Memoranda to", ah, "Silenus".'

'And it won?'

'Indeed yes.'

Bysouth grinned like a wolf.

'I cannot tell you how deeply we regret this blunder. Naturally none of the judges remembered the poem as one of your early works.'

'Philistines,' said Bysouth. 'Judges, critics, the lowest form of life. What would they remember? What have they ever written that is worth remembering? Who were the judges?'

'Mr Gavin Jarvis was on the panel, and Mr –'

'Jarvis isn't a poet. A good televison performer, a smart dresser, a ladies' man. But a pseud, a phoney. He must go and sit with the Professor of Poetry and we shall ignore them both.'

'As you wish,' said Bacon. 'But this has left us with rather an embarrassing matter on our hands. The announcement about the prizewinners has already appeared in the press and it would be highly unfortunate if we were to disclose that we had been, er, hoaxed. It would generate the most unwelcome publicity, particularly since we do feel that the image of the tobacco industry is vulnerable to attack at the moment in view of the public's attitude towards smoking. Of course, there is also the potential embarrassment for you. You will, of course, feel justifiably outraged.' Bacon thought he had perhaps put it a little strongly. 'Justifiably upset,' he said, on second thoughts.

'Well, well,' said Bysouth. 'I'm surprised that it won. As a matter of fact not many people in England have read that poem. I would say about ten, or maybe fourteen.'

'Well, of course, a great many people have read it now. It was published in all the papers as the winning poem.'

'Was it?' said Bysouth. 'We'll have another drink on that.' He looked at the remains of Bacon's fiver lying on the table. Hastily Bacon produced another note.

'Who sent my poem in for the competition?'

'We do not know the identity of the person. This is a source of considerable distress to us, as you can imagine. The imposter simply signed himself J. W. Blanks.'

Bysouth worked his jaws vigorously. 'J. W. Blanks?'

'I'm afraid so.'

'I'm sure that is the name of the Professor of Poetry,' said Bysouth, starting to laugh. 'If not, then it ought to be.' He finished the whisky. Then he laughed again. 'Well, how can I help you?' he said, laughing so much now that his red-rimmed eyes began to stream. He produced a handkerchief which contained particles of doubtful matter. Like a maiden lady, Bacon averted his eyes.

'We are reluctant to call off the entire competition,' he said slowly. 'Profiles of the winners are to be written, *Sparkle!* magazine is bringing a coach party of readers to the presentation, the Mayor of Banting has agreed to be present. Now, obviously, since one of the winners does not exist, he cannot be interviewed. What I would propose is that we, as it were, do away with him, quietly and informally. I would make a statement to the press saying, that Mr Blanks is unwilling to be interviewed. Then things could go ahead as planned and the ceremony could proceed without him.'

'What about the money?' said Bysouth, opening his eyes rather wide. His manner, it seemed to Bacon, had imperceptibly changed.

'What money?'

'The prize money. Who is going to get it?'

'Well, we would make a donation to charity, or perhaps share the amount among the runners-up. I haven't given the matter much thought.'

'I can think of a suitable charity,' said Bysouth, heaving with mirth.

'Excellent,' said Bacon. 'Oxfam? Help the Aged? Or is there a cause you particularly favour?'

'The Bysouth Foundation.'

'Ah yes, what is that?' said Bacon, who was beginning to be affected by the whisky.

'Myself. You can give the money to me.'

Bacon regarded him with extreme distaste. It was repulsive to be confronted with such an openly grasping nature.

'I'll take the money and keep quiet about the whole thing,' said Bysouth. 'Trust me. After all, since it was my poem that won, I'm entitled to the cash. I'll be J. W. Blanks's representative.' He stumbled slightly over the word. 'You can tell everyone he's too retiring to speak to the press, but that I, as a close friend, am acting on his behalf. I will accept the prize for him, by proxy. A short speech would be in order?'

'I shall have to refer this matter to the chairman, Mr Bysouth. He's a very important man. I can't just go around giving you large amounts of money and letting you make speeches. He may not like it. He may give poor old Bacon a slap on the wrist.'

'Another whisky?'

Bacon retraced his steps uncertainly towards the bar.

'Cheers.'

'Cheers. I would attend the ceremony?' said Bysouth with some excitement. 'All expenses paid? Good hotel? Slap up dinner for two?'

Bacon leaned forward and stared into Bysouth's clouded eyes. 'All the trimmings,' he said. It really was pathetic. Money was all the wretched old man cared about. 'The cash, the hotel, the expenses, the speech,' he said, 'on condition that you keep quiet.'

'Not a word to any living man.'

A middle-aged woman came over to Bacon. 'Are you lonely, dear. Would you like some company?'

'Fuck off,' said Bysouth.

'Pardon me for living,' she said and went away.

'Silly tart,' said Bysouth. 'Let's have another drink.'

'An excellent idea.'

'Here's to the Professor of Poetry.'

'Cheers.'

'Cheers.'

A man in a flowered shirt came up and greeted

Bysouth. It was the same man, Bacon saw with horror, who had been playing cards at the Spanking Cinema. 'Hello again,' the man said, winking at Bacon in a knowing way. He touched Bysouth on the elbow. 'Who's your friend?'

'Cigarette man,' said Bysouth. 'Just your type.'

'You do get about,' the man with the wooden leg said admiringly to Bacon. 'Where do you come from?'

'Berkeley Square,' said Bacon, pronouncing his words with difficulty. The air was acrid with the fumes of tobacco and alcohol. Bacon squinted at his watch. It was five-thirty already. Doreen would be waiting at the station in the car.

'I say, I think I must be making a move.'

'Oh, don't go yet. Just when we were getting to know each other.'

'He'll buy us both another drink if we ask him nicely,' said Bysouth. 'His funds are unlimited.'

Wearily Bacon bought them all another drink.

'Do you like art?' said the man with the wooden leg. 'Photographic art of unusual scenes?'

Bacon watched Bysouth's nose as it began to run. The poet clutched his arm. 'Do you think you could let me have it in writing? Adrian here can be a witness.'

'To what?'

'The deal. Would you like to confirm the details on paper?'

'I've never been attracted to women,' said Adrian, 'but I don't want you to think it's because of the leg, because that's got nothing to do with it.'

'He got it in the war,' said Bysouth.

'Fighting for King and country.'

'Well done,' said Bacon. He rose carefully to his feet. 'If you would excuse me, I must leave you now. The contract will be with you in the morning, if that is agreeable to you.' He walked unsteadily towards the door. He thought with longing of his usual train, his empty seat occupied now by a surprised stranger, gratified at finding an unexpected place. He thought of his wife sitting angrily in the car park as the commuters disembarked and he was not among them. He thought of Cheryl, but at this bleak visions rose up before him. He wandered out into the night, steering an erratic and unhappy course for Waterloo Station. The air outside was cold and damp. He looked in vain for a taxi and stepped out abruptly into the road as one approached, but it swerved away from him and disappeared at high speed.

'I was nearly killed,' said Bacon, swaying on the spot. The world spun; he was dazzled. A woman stood beside him waiting to cross the road. Drunkenly he smiled into her face.

'Would you care for a good time, madam?' he said.

'Not with you, you ugly old toad,' she said, stepping angrily away.

Bacon continued to walk with difficulty in the direction of the railway station.

'Did you see that wretched fellow?' said Walter Dove as the taxi swung round Piccadilly Circus. 'We almost knocked him down. He stepped off the pavement quite without warning. Obviously drunk.'

'He seemed rather smartly dressed,' said Nina Cleverly.

'That's true of a lot of these dropouts. Alcoholics, of course. It's a depressing business.'

The taxi sped along, spun round Hyde Park Corner and then lurched towards Belgravia. In the darkness of its interior Dove took Nina Cleverly's hand. The streets grew narrower and elegant white facades shone out from the darkness, their white porticoes illuminated by carefully placed spotlights.

Dove's hand was soft and moist. 'I'm so terribly pleased you're writing this article,' he said, leaning towards her. 'So often they send someone who has no interest at all in the subject, whereas I can tell that you are a very sensitive person. You're a listener. You let people talk, and you listen to what they say which, believe me, is very, very rare among women. Very rare indeed.'

'Is it?'

'Yes. You're a very special woman,' said Dove, letting his free hand stray over her shoulder. 'I'm so glad we've met. Aren't you glad we've met?'

'Yes.'

'Really glad?'

'Yes.'

The taxi stopped at the Terpsichore Club where Gavin Jarvis was, at that very moment, getting out of another taxi.

'Walter, hi!' he said, waving at them.

'How are you, Gavin?'

'Fine. How are things?'

'Fine. And with you?'

'Oh, fine.'

The premises of the Club were striking and monumental. They went up white marble steps into an airy vestibule where a large crowd was moving slowly through a pair of heavy oak doors. As the guests arrived waiters offered sherry, which they drank quickly hoping their glasses would be refilled.

'Dry or medium?' Dove asked Nina Cleverly.

'Dry,' said Jarvis, standing behind Dove. He was wearing a dark grey suit with an open-necked white shirt and expensive white running shoes. As Dove fussed over the drinks, Jarvis tipped back his head and stared at Nina Cleverly. After some time he dropped his eyes from her face and coolly appraised the rest of her body.

'Are you on your own?' said Dove in irritation as Jarvis continued to stare at Nina. 'Where's . . .' He attempted to remember the name of one of Jarvis's girl-friends.

'Hey, Walter,' said Jarvis, smiling slightly. 'Has *Advance* folded at last?'

'Of course not,' said Dove. 'It's doing remarkably well. Why?'

Jarvis snapped his fingers in Dove's face. 'No cheque,' he said.

'For what?'

'Bender. A new appraisal.'

'Did we use the piece?'

'Naturally.'

'Well, your cheque should have arrived. I'm sure it will be in the post.'

'That's all right then,' said Jarvis. He smiled faintly.

'Good.'

'Right.'

Since Jarvis continued to contemplate them, Dove touched Nina's elbow and steered her through the oak doors into a small, crowded hall where chairs had been arranged in a semi-circle round a raised platform. The atmosphere was melancholy despite the low, excited murmur of the guests. From stained-glass windows which extended along the length of one wall, elaborately dressed muses looked down patronisingly, displaying scrolls with improving legends. 'Knowledge now no more a fountain sealed,' declared one banner, and 'Praise him with the sound of the sackbut.'

Dove attempted to find them seats near the front. 'They serve more drinks after the talk,' he said to Nina Cleverly. 'After we've all asked questions.'

'It sounds very interesting,' she said, taking out a note-book.

'There are lots of people here you might care to meet. I'll introduce you to them afterwards. I'm sure it will add some atmosphere to your piece. Look, Nina,' – Dove's voice dropped to a whisper – 'I'm sorry I didn't introduce you just now to Gavin Jarvis. He's fine in small doses, but not one of my dearest friends. I found it awfully depressing the way he raised the business of that cheque. He earns more than anyone I know from his books, his Arts Council money and his television series, and yet there he was, whining on about his payment from *Advance*. As if it makes any diffference to him. I think it's sad to see someone so mercenary, and I've often found that people with money are terribly petty. Frankly Nina, I might as well tell you, I think he's the most frightful –'

A light tap on his shoulder made Dove start nervously. Jarvis was sitting directly behind them, his feet carefully arranged on an adjacent chair. 'Do I know you?' he asked Nina.

'May I introduce Nina Cleverly,' said Dove in a remote voice. 'She's preparing an article about poetry for *Sparkle!* magazine.'

Jarvis looked at Nina but did not extend his hand.

'Women's magazine?'

'Yes, but we are keen to extend our coverage of the arts.' Jarvis leaned back and lit a cigarette. 'Why don't you write about me,' he said. 'I'm much more interesting than Walter, who isn't a poet at all. Are you Walter?'

'Good heavens, she isn't writing about me,' said Dove. 'Whatever gave you that idea?'

'I believe I have seen you on television,' said Nina Cleverly.

'How is the series going?' said Dove in annoyance.

' "Poets in a Landscape"?' said Jarvis. 'It's top of the ratings. It's a hit.'

'I must watch it some time,' said Dove. 'You go on television quite a lot, don't you?'

'Yes,' said Jarvis. 'It's a real drag. I only do the programmes that really interest me now, or I'd have no time for my writing.'

'No,' said Dove, who had only broadcast on the radio. 'Of course, many people would argue that the wireless is a more sympathetic medium to poetry.'

'Right,' said Jarvis. 'But the money . . .' He shrugged his shoulders with an expression of disgust.

The audience was now seated expectantly on the uncomfortable chairs. Jarvis started talking to a man sitting next to him whose head was completely bald. As the audience talked to each other in a low murmur of anticipation, an extremely thin man walked with apparent difficulty onto the platform and there was a burst of encouraging applause. Long greasy hair curled round his neck and littered his jacket with a light crust of dandruff. His skin was yellow and his face cadaverous.

Dove whispered to Nina. 'That's A. N. W. S. Savory. He's going to tell us about Robert Bantam. He was a very close friend.'

The applause died away. A. N. W. S. Savory cleared his throat with a high, reedy cough.

'Robert Bantam once said to me,' he said in a light, rapid voice, 'that he lived in quite another world from that of the ordinary man, and I have always believed that to be the most important clue to understanding his life and work. For the perceptions of the poet are, in a very real sense, not of our world. Through his mysterious art the common-place and the pedestrian become transmuted into the extraordinary and the sublime. The poet's world is the same as ours, and yet it is different. It is the world of the senses, and yet it is not. I shall try to tell you what made his friends regard Bantam as a man so remarkable in so many ways.

'I first met Robert Bantam when we were up at Oxford together . . .'

Jarvis groaned loudly and whispered something. Dove turned round and made a sibilant complaint. Oblivious of the interuption, A. N. W. S. Savory continued: 'At the time when I met him, Bantam was a young classical scholar of a prodigious and outstanding talent. Though most of his contemporaries would amuse themselves in the diversions of the time – on the river, at the theatre, or, I am afraid, in the college bars – Bantam's especial pleasure was to address himself, as a means of relaxation, to the task of translating the works of T. S. Eliot into Greek lyric verse. Not an easy task I can assure you. Many were the evenings when we would see his light burning as we stood there out on the quad, and many were the occasions when we would exclaim, "Look, there is Robert Bantam translating *Four Quartets* into Greek Alcaics." I well remember one night, when we returned hilarious from some college supper . . .'

A. N. W. S. Savory spoke on in a shrill and monotonous voice. Nina Cleverly took notes.

'. . . and he would say to me, "I believe I have discovered

a word for 'photograph album' thanks to the unplumbed depths of the Greek language." Many were the evenings we spent together, engaged in the pursuit of the elusive.'

A. N. W. S. Savory spoke for some time. At intervals, Dove would turn from his seat to address Gavin Jarvis, imploring him to stop interrupting with constant whispers or sudden barks of suppressed laughter. At a particularly loud outburst from Jarvis a woman in one of the back rows waved her arm, with a jangle of bracelets, and hissed, 'Shut up, Gavin.'

Nina Cleverly turned to see the woman more clearly. She had a great quantity of black, spiky hair and wore a red, Indian skirt decorated with silver mirrors. She had an air of sophistication and her bright, black eyes stared out confidently into the crowded room.

'Who is that?'

Dove nervously turned to look. 'Eva Vandriver.'

'She's very attractive.'

'If you like that sort of thing. I don't personally care much for it myself.'

The speaker came to a halt. In the silence that followed no one was sure if he had finished his speech or was simply pausing for a rest. Eva Vandriver brought the uncertainty to an end by bursting into loud applause. Taking up the cue, the rest of the audience began to clap and A. N. W. S. Savory decided to call it a day. He was helped to a chair on the platform and a small man in spectacles came onto the stage and made a perfunctory speech of thanks. Then he asked them all to raise their questions. 'Mr Savory is pleased to answer any points you might like to take up with him,' he said.

There was a prolonged and uneasy silence, while members of the audience coughed in embarrassment. Eva Vandriver stood up. 'I wonder if Mr Savory could tell us whether he thinks Robert Bantam is, in the last analysis, a romantic or a classical poet,' she said.

The audience regarded her with admiration.

'I apologise for not rising to my feet,' said A. N. W. S Savory, 'but I am under doctor's orders to take things easy. The point about Bantam is that he was in one very real sense a romantic, but then again in the light of his respect for form and tradition, he certainly could not be inaccurately described as writing in the classical style . . .'

He spoke for another ten minutes. When, eventually, he stopped, the audience eyed each other, wondering if anyone would risk another question. In the end the attraction of alcohol was stronger. They escaped into the library where a fire burned cheerfully and drinks were arranged on a large table.

'What an enjoyable talk,' said the bald man to Dove as they filed towards the table in an orderly queue.

'Yes, most stimulating,' said Dove, although Nina had seen him yawn towards the end of Savory's address. 'May I introduce –' but Gavin Jarvis had come up to them again.

'Stimulating?' he said challengingly to Dove. 'Personally I would question what stimulus Savory's reminiscences have for anyone writing poetry today. Tedious reflections about life at Oxford, in-jokes about the literary establishment, the initiates of the academy closing their ranks, dedicated to upholding the cultural values of a self-perpetuating, self-congratulatory oligarchy of taste? Frankly his whole ideology is dead as a dodo.'

Dove move ineffectually towards the drinks table, but Jarvis continued to harangue him.

'– is exclusivity in art,' he said. 'What have we provided tonight except the vapid meanderings of a washed-up, geriatric don. What about an acknowledgement of a whole new generation of writers working in alternative areas of literary experience? I mean poets working in community groups, in workshops, exploring the untapped creativity of an economically under-privileged but nevertheless highly vocal section of the population instead of massaging the egos of a self-approbating élite. Writers who are exploring the fabric of language by working out its meaning in –'

Dove reached the drinks table and secured two

glasses of wine. 'I wouldn't pay too much attention to Jarvis, if I were you,' he said to Nina. 'Of course, I don't want to tell you what to write, but it is believed that his ideas are a little bit unsound. He went to public school and Oxford himself, you know, although in his proletarian mood he'll say anything.'

Dove glanced about the room. He seemed ill at ease and, Nina observed, had a hunted expression. She had just taken her first sip of wine when he seized her elbow and began to push her in the direction of the door.

'I think we've heard just about enough here, don't you?' he said hastily. 'I think we might move on to something a little more exciting for you.'

'But what about the poets?'

'Who?'

'You said you were going to introduce me to many interesting figures in the world of poetry.'

'Yes,' said Dove. 'Yes, but I think you could talk to them at, er, greater length in a more intimate setting. After all, it's very hard for you to make notes here isn't it, with all these people talking at once. Anyway, there's no one really interesting here.'

'Oh.'

'I'll find some much more interesting people for you,' said Dove, pushing her harder towards the door. As they neared the exit, Nina saw Eva Vandriver waving at Dove in what seemed a rather sarcastic manner. Dove ignored her. Jarvis had found someone else to talk to.

'A fantastic, defiantly joyous experience,' he was saying. 'The whole carriage became an act of spontaneous theatre, with the commuters participating in the ritual. It's called Tube Theatre. It urges a concept of a truly democratic aesthetic, since audience and actors are equally privileged celebrants in the ceremony.'

Nina Cleverly watched Eva Vandriver go up to Jarvis and touch his cheek lightly. 'Hello, stranger,' she said. 'I haven't seen you for weeks. What have you been doing with yourself.'

'I'm a writer in residence at the Porson Institute this

year,' said Jarvis. 'Term's just started. I've been pretty busy talking to the students.'

'Look,' said Eva Vandriver, 'why don't we –'

But Nina heard no more as Dove pulled her through the door and out into the street. He hailed a taxi. Inside he loosened his tie and seemed to relax.

'Did you enjoy that, Nina?'

'Very much.'

'I'm sorry we had to rush away rather quickly.'

'Not at all.'

'It's just that well, to be frank, you probably noticed that rather loudly dressed woman, Eva Vandriver, waving and staring at me. Well, the thing is – it's very upsetting for me to tell you this – but the thing is, I happen to be married. In fact I am married to her.'

'To Eva Vandriver?'

'Yes. The thing is, Nina, that I didn't particularly want to start a scene in there. She can be quite ridiculously temperamental and I didn't want her to cause any trouble, especially with you trying to get material for your article. I wanted you to enjoy yourself.'

'Do you live together?'

'Well, in the same house, yes. But you could hardly call it living together. It's a mere formality. No one could call our relationship a marriage, just a mockery for two people living together at the same address. I don't really want to talk about it, Nina, not with you here, like this. You see, I wanted things to be different. I feel you're a very sensitive person and that you can perhaps understand how I feel. Eva and I are like two strangers. In fact, things started to go wrong almost as soon as we were married . . .'

Walter Dove's hand lay smooth and damp in hers as the taxi sped through the quiet night and he talked softly and insistently, explaining in some detail exactly why it was that his wife had failed to understand him.

5

Eddie Rosemary sat in his silent house in Appletree Crescent and waited for the *Sparkle!* reporter to arrive. He looked round the austere sitting room, trying to see it with a stranger's eye, fearful that its lack of decoration – the worn three-piece suite, walls unrelieved by pictures, the absence of ornament – might betray some unsuspected intimacy to a curious onlooker. He had already locked his diaries and letters away in a portable file, believing that the reporter might surreptitiously investigate his drawers while his back was turned.

As a concession to social convention he had cleared a space in the middle of the room by pushing his accumulated piles of newspaper cuttings, poetry pamphlets and magazines to the outer edges of the carpet. They lay there on unsteady foundations, threatening at any moment to surge in a yellowing flood back to their accustomed places.

Rosemary's mouth was dry. He had never before spoken to anyone about his poetry. It was a secret at the dark, guarded core of his life. He confided in no one; he had no friends apart from his cheerful and incurious colleagues in the accounts department of Cartons (UK) Ltd, with whom he cordially grumbled about their conditions of employment. To talk about himself would be, at once, disconcerting and thrilling, for his diffidence contended with his desire to be recognised. After years of harsh self-discipline, of practising his art in insolation, he now found himself fighting a hysterical desire to confide in the expected stranger, to throw himself open for

71

inspection, to be acknowledged, admired and accepted.

The minutes passed slowly. Rosemary walked over to the window and gazed down the empty street. He forced himself to sit for exactly a minute on the sofa while his heart raced. It seemed that his goal was actually within reach. That he might be read, by *Sparkle!* readers, by publishers, by other poets; that he might be published. That a book might one day exist consisting of his collected works, something tangible, some record of the years of work. 'Fame is not important,' said Rosemary, but in his heart he knew that fame did matter to him. He wanted to win the praise of his masters, he wanted the victor's palm. He believed himself to be a great poet and he longed to move easily in that inaccessible world where poets knew and greeted each other. These desires, he knew, were dangerous. They were distracting and seductive. But here, as he waited for the press in his ugly home, he knew they had utterly overcome his sterner resolutions.

The afternoon light was growing weak. Soon it would be too late to take photographs. Rosemary went to the window again. As he looked down the uniform rows of cypresses he suddenly saw a car coming down the road. There were two people inside it. It was an old, rather battered car, not the sort he imagined the press would use, but all the same it was advancing towards him. Rosemary saw someone leaning out of the passenger window, counting the numbers on the houses. Here were without any doubt, his visitors.

He moved quickly away from the window. He heard car doors slam and his doorbell shrill. He had a sudden sense that whatever might happen now was somehow fixed and inevitable. He opened the door.

Nina Cleverly smiled coldly and extended her hand. Rosemary touched it carefully 'I am the *Sparkle!* reporter. This is our photographer, Lord Broubster.'

'How are you?' said Lord Broubster, who was wearing a safari suit despite the inclement weather.

Surprised by the unexpected presence of nobility

Rosemary bent to carry Lord Broubster's bag of photographic equipment over the threshold.

'It's quite all right,' said Lord Broubster, 'I can manage it.'

'Let me give you a hand.'

'No need –' As they dived together for the bag their heads cracked sharply above it. 'So sorry,' said Lord Broubster, crouching on the floor.

Rosemary jerked at the bag and Lord Broubster relinquished it. He carried it triumphantly into the sitting room, staggering a little beneath its weight. Rosemary gestured towards Nina Cleverly, inviting her to sit on his sofa. He dared not risk words with her yet. The *Sparkle!* team stepped with some difficulty across the litter of papers. 'What a jolly place!' said Lord Broubster. 'And so convenient for the motorway.'

'And the railway station,' said Rosemary. Lord Broubster did not reply but contented himself with screwing together pieces of his camera.

'Would you like some tea?' said Rosemary, moving towards the kitchen.

'I think we should start straight away with the photographs,' said Nina Cleverly, 'while the light is still strong enough.'

'All right,' said Rosemary and sat down on the sofa.

'We'll go outside,' said Lord Broubster.

Rosemary stood up again.

'Is there a particular spot where you like to go,' said Nina Cleverly. 'The sort of place that gives you inspiration?'

'I don't believe in inspiration very much,' said Rosemary. 'It's no good sitting around waiting to be inspired if you have to do your job during the day and write in the evenings. You waste a lot of time that way. I just sit down and use whatever is there, whether I feel inspired or not.'

'Well, somewhere you go to walk and look at nature?'

'I'm not particularly interested in nature,' said Rosemary.

His visitors walked uneasily round the bleak room. 'Well, just somewhere with a few trees,' said Lord Broubster. 'I don't want anything too obvious, but the outside of your house isn't too promising.'

'There's a place I go to sometimes in the morning, to make observations. Purely as a technical exercise. It isn't important to me.'

'Sounds fine,' said Lord Broubster. 'Just the job.'

He took them down to the fields under the motorway, through the thistles to an area of marsh where cows had recently waded. Nina Cleverly was wearing unsuitable shoes.

'I usually wear Wellingtons,' said Rosemary.

'It doesn't matter,' said Nina Cleverly, stepping carefully. With some difficulty she followed with her notebook as Rosemary and Lord Broubster went ahead through a barbed wire fence into a field which was desolate in its wintry coverings of sparse, yellowish grass.

'What is your poetry about?' said Nina Cleverly, feeling she might as well make a start.

'It's hard to describe,' said Rosemary. 'The best thing would be to read some of it, or I could read some to you, if you liked.'

'Well, that would be very helpful at some point. I wonder though if you could just sum up the themes that interest you. For example, do you write about political subjects, or war, or do you prefer love poems?'

'It's hard to say.'

'Do try.'

'Well, I write about all kinds of different things. I can't really sum them up like . . . Do you want me to look at you?'

'Just go ahead,' said Lord Broubster. 'I'll catch you as you talk. Do carry on about your poems. They sound fascinating.'

Nina Cleverly smiled at him encouragingly. 'When did you first start writing poetry?'

'When I was about twelve,' said Rosemary. 'But I wouldn't call it poetry, it was . . .' Watching Nina

Cleverly transfer his words to her notebook had a paralysing effect. He found himself incapable of coherent speech.

'Are you writing everything down?'

'Yes.'

'Just as I say it?'

'Yes. Don't worry, I'll turn it into English for you.'

'Thank you,' said Rosemary.

'Just forget about the camera and the notebook and tell us how you became a poet.'

Rosemary swallowed desperately. The interview was far worse than anything he had imagined.

'Was there some special event that triggered you off,' said Nina Cleverly, 'or did you always want to be a poet?'

'I suppose all events are triggers,' said Rosemary, 'in a subsconscious way. What happens to you is bound to influence what you become. I suppose that isn't very helpful.'

'I know how difficult it must be talking to strangers,' said Nina Cleverly, looking with irritation at the short paragraph she had so far collected. 'But our readers would be interested to know how you began. It might be helpful to them.'

'How could you help someone to be a poet?' said Rosemary. 'Either you'd be one, or you wouldn't. I shouldn't think reading a magazine article would make much difference.'

'It might encourage them.'

'Reading about me?'

'Yes. Did anyone encourage you?'

'No.'

'Where were you born?'

'Harlow New Town.'

'Did you enjoy school?'

'No.'

'Did you go to university?'

'No.'

'And now you work for Cartons (UK) Ltd?'

'In the finance department.'

'That must be very interesting work.'

'As a matter of fact,' said Rosemary, 'there is nothing interesting about my job at all.'

There was a short silence as Lord Broubster took a succession of rapid shots. They walked a little further towards the motorway tunnel.

'What an unexpected place to find these fields,' said Nina Cleverly, looking up at the motorway. 'What made you decide to live here?'

'The houses are quite cheap. It only takes half an hour to get to London.'

'It's quite unusual for a literary person to live in Slough, isn't it?'

'Is it unusual? I didn't know that. But I wouldn't say that I was a literary person. I hope you won't write that down about me.'

Nina Cleverly suspended the movement of her pencil.

'You're not a literary person?'

'No,' said Rosemary. 'Not at all. I'm a poet.'

'Could you just look at the camera?' said Lord Broubster. 'Just stay like that for a moment. Fine. Now, just carry on talking to Nina.'

'What about your parents?' said Nina wearily.

'They are rather old.'

'Do they like poetry?'

'Oh, they don't read books. Just the *TV Times* and *Titbits*.'

Nina's pencil came to a halt again. Rosemary felt a surge of panic. Clearly there was nothing about him that she found interesting. She would go away and possibly report that he was not worth writing about. He tried to interest her.

'There is never a moment,' he said, pointing to the motorway, 'when the cars actually stop. Of course, if they did it would mean –'

'Walk over here please,' said Lord Broubster. 'I want to use a filter in these next shots.'

'What kind of camera do you use?'

'Helsinki.'

'I've been thinking of buying a camera myself recently. You're just the sort of person to ask for advice.'

'Look at the cows,' said Lord Broubster. 'Do you think you could be writing a poem in this next picture?'

Rosemary looked at him sympathetically. 'If you like.'

'Would you like a piece of paper?' said Nina Cleverly.

'I have my notebook,' said Rosemary, pulling a small book from his jacket pocket. He held it before his face with an expression of concentration.

'Super,' said Lord Broubster.

'Do you write every evening after work?' asked Nina Cleverly. 'And what about weekends?'

Eddie Rosemary stared at his notebook and chewed his lips. He did not reply. He started to write several words down in his book then he crossed them out again. He stared down at the page and wrote some more words with a slight frown. Nina repeated the question rather more loudly. Still he did not reply. She struck him briskly on the arm. 'Look, there's no need for you to write real poetry for the photograph. Just write rubbish, or a nursery rhyme.'

'I'm sorry,' said Rosemary. 'I was just thinking about something. I'll write out a poem I already know, shall I?'

'Fine.'

He copied some lines into the notebook. Lord Broubster took some more pictures then he stopped.

'I say,' he said, 'those cows are coming nearer.'

The herd was indeed approaching, moving softly through the mist. From the tunnel under the motorway several more came to join them until the field was a mass of slowly moving bovine life. The cows advanced to the barbed wire fence which separated them from the *Sparkle!* team and the poet. They stared curiously at the trio, their tails perpetually flicking in the fading light.

Lord Broubster regarded the cows with interest and began to photograph them. Nina Cleverly turned to him in some alarm. 'I believe the cows are being driven. There appears to be someone with them.'

Sure enough, a distant figure was advancing out of the mist towards them.

'Is this private land?' said Nina Cleverly.

'Very likely,' said Rosemary.

Lord Broubster began to gather his equipment together.

'No need to worry,' said Rosemary, but the *Sparkle!* team were hastily gathering up their belongings.

'He's got a gun,' said Nina Cleverly, her voice rising with hysteria.

'Is he aiming it?' said Lord Broubster shrilly, preparing for flight.

'It's the farmer,' said Rosemary. 'I suppose we're in his field.'

In silence they gazed at the approaching figure. Lord Broubster cleared his throat. 'Leave him to me,' he said in a whisper. 'I'll get my cheque book out if he shows any sign of trouble.'

The farmer stared at them with no sign of friendliness.

'Good afternoon,' shrieked Lord Broubster. 'I hope you will forgive us for intruding upon your land briefly, but I am in fact Lord Broubster and I am photographing Mr Rosemary here for *Sparkle!* magazine. It's for an article about poetry. Perhaps you would like us to send you a complimentary copy?'

The farmer continued to stare at them.

'If he goes for the gun,' whispered Nina Cleverly, 'tell him that *Sparkle!* will sue for assault. We are heavily insured.'

Then the farmer moved. He reached into his pocket and brought out a dirty scrap of paper. 'Will you sign this?' he said to Lord Broubster. 'The wife collects autographs. She'd like to have yours, sir.'

'Delighted,' said Lord Broubster, scrawling on the paper. The farmer passed it to Nina Cleverly, who signed too. Rosemary took out his pen, but she gave the paper back to the farmer. He nodded at the *Sparkle!* representatives. 'Good afternoon.' Slowly he passed them, driving the cows before him.

'Well,' said Nina Cleverly, 'what a relief! I thought he was going to shoot us dead.'

'A decent sort of chap,' said Lord Broubster. 'I think he was rather thrilled to meet us, you know. It means a lot to these people to talk to someone rather well known. He'll be able to tell his wife all about it.'

The interview showed signs of coming to an end. Dissatisfied with his performance, Rosemary invited them back to his house. 'There is champagne in the fridge,' he said. 'Will you share my celebration?'

The mist now obscured the boundaries of the field from view. The air was raw and damp. 'After you,' said Rosemary. Haltingly they proceeded back to the car where Nina and Lord Broubster congratulated each other on accomplishing their mission like explorers regaining the safety of camp.

'This is where I sleep,' said Rosemary unnecessarily. Nina Cleverly and Lord Broubster stared at the double bed standing in the centre of the cold, blue room. There were some mugs on the floor, half full of grey liquid. Rosemary looked at this evidence of his domestic life with detached annoyance. He hoped Nina would not mention the items in the article.

They passed silently to the adjacent room. It was smaller than the bedroom and its walls were completely screened by cheap, collapsible bookcases, filled with a great many paperback books. The desk, which occupied almost all of the floor space, was arranged with great precision in a neat formation of pencils, rubbers, a pencil sharpener and a stop-watch.

'Your study?' said Nina.

Rosemary nodded.

'It is very tidy.'

'Organisation is important. The artist, as Auden said, is living in a state of siege. Only clarity and economy will work against the void.'

Their tour of the house completed, they followed him downstairs and into the sitting room. He filled their glasses with champagne. Nina Cleverly stared gloomily at her notebook. He had said very little, she thought, and nothing at all of any consequence.

'Why did you decide to go in for the competition?'

Rosemary leaned forward and clasped his hands together. His knuckles were white as he fought his own fastidious shrinking from self-exposure and a fierce desire to fill Nina Cleverly's under-used notebook. Eventually he looked up.

'I knew it was the right moment.'

'The right moment?'

'I knew I could win. I knew I had to test myself against the other competitors. And I knew that if I didn't win I would probably give it all up.'

'All your writing?'

'Yes. You get to the point where you can't go on working in a vacuum. I had to put myself to the test. It's all part of the plan.'

'What plan?'

'To be a great poet.'

Her pencil began to move more quickly. Hesitatingly, then growing in confidence, Rosemary told her about the pattern he had devised for his life, confiding those furtive, breathless aspirations he had cherished for so many years. He told her about his decision to live alone, to eliminate all distractions from his life, to do nothing but work, driving on into the unknown darkness. 'After a while,' he said, 'it becomes almost intoxicating. To come home every night to solitude, to leave the train, the commuters, all the ugly women, and to sit alone in an empty house working on and on, sometimes until two or three in the morning. I believed I had to prepare myself since I was eventually going to face some great trial. And now – the competition. It's what I have been working towards. Don't you see that I have spent my life preparing for it?'

'Don't you ever feel you want to go out and enjoy yourself?'

'There's no time,' said Rosemary. 'And besides, I don't much like crowds. I'd rather be here on my own. I was sixteen when I left school – please don't put that in the article – and I was quite good at mathematics, but nothing else. So I was lucky to get into Cartons (UK) Ltd, in the accounts department.'

Nina Cleverly listened, writing all the time in her notebook. Her attention flattered him. He became garrulous, recklessly confiding to her what he had never told anyone before. ' "I find that I cannot exist without poetry." That's what Keats said. There is nothing more important to me. I don't even mind working at Cartons (UK) Ltd. I think poets should know about the ordinary lives most people lead.'

A slight sound made him turn his head. Lord Broubster, his glass balanced precariously on the chair, had fallen asleep. His mouth was slightly open and he breathed through it. 'The day has been too much for him,' said Nina Cleverly. 'He was photographing models in swimsuits at six o'clock this morning. He works very hard.'

'I suppose I just want to explain,' said Rosemary, 'that winning the competition has made everything worthwhile. I've never had a chance to meet other poets. That's the hardest thing, to go on and on and not be certain that there's any point to it at all.'

'It must have been difficult,' said Nina Cleverly.

'Yes.'

She looked surreptitiously at her watch. Lord Broubster slid gradually down his chair until his head had slipped forward onto his chest.

The *Sparkle!* readers still needed one more piece of information.

'Is there anyone special,' said Nina Cleverly, 'in your life at the moment?'

'What?' said Rosemary.

'Do you live alone . . . ?'

He looked round the room, not understanding.

'I mean, do you have a girlfriend?'

Rosemary flinched. 'No,' he said, blushing in embarrassment. 'I suppose it would make your article much more interesting if I did. I'm afraid you haven't got much to write about.'

'There's plenty of material,' said Nina Cleverly, snapping her notebook shut. She got up and went to look at Lord Broubster.

'More champagne?' said Eddie Rosemary, desperate that the interview seemed to be at an end. But she did not reply. Bending over Lord Broubster she shook him gently by the shoulder.

'Book the studio for seven o'clock sharp,' he said, waking instantly. 'Thank you so much, Mr Rosemary, for such an enjoyable afternoon.' He looked about him as if uncertain where he was.

'Another drink before you go?' said Rosemary.

Lord Broubster rose in a fluid movement from the depths of the chair. 'Good luck with your writing,' he said. 'A most stimulating conversation.'

They left him alone in the still house.

Standing at the window, Rosemary saw the car drive away. Half drunk, he walked unsteadily into the small, untended garden and watched until he could no longer see the lights from the car. Returning to the sitting room he swallowed another glass of champagne. He wondered what Nina Cleverly would write about him.

Rosemary remembered his notebook and took it from his jacket pocket. There were scribbled words, the notes he had made while he was posing for Lord Broubster. He took out his pencil but the alcohol had confused him. He could only see Nina's face, stern and questioning; he could only relive his own muddled answers.

On the next page of his notebook he saw the verse he had copied out from memory:

O plunge your hands in water,
Plunge them in up to the wrist;
Stare, stare in the basin
And wonder what you've missed.

The glacier knocks in the cupboard,
The desert sighs in the bed,

And the crack in the teacup opens
    A lane to the land of the dead.

Grief and disappointment overwhelmed him. A precious opportunity had been missed. He went to the photograph on the television set, his only concession to decoration. Kneeling before it he stared into the smiling face, trying to recover those perceptions of a more vivid world which he had forgotten and would go on forgetting.

6

Violet Glasspool noted that her curtains needed cleaning. Then as she sat staring at the stained and splashed velvet drapery she saw further evidence of neglect which distressed her. The windows were opaque with grime; dust lay heavily over the bookcase and on the desk there was a quantity of soiled crockery – plates, cups and crusted forks – as though a person of slovenly habits had taken more than one meal there.

Violet moved over to the desk with the intention of clearing away the crockery, wondering to herself how it had got there. She saw that the desk top was awash with paper of an astonishing variety, some of it white and crisp, some yellowing and creased, all covered with a layer of powdery dust. From the profusion upon the desk she reached for a sheet of clean white paper. Meticulously she filled her fountain pen and blotted it.

Dear Mr Rosemary, she wrote. As one of the judges of the Coote & Balding Poetry Competition I thought I would just drop you a note to say well done, and express my hopes that you will carry on writing. I don't know your name, or whether you have been published, but it is always delightful to discover someone new and talented. You seem to me to have a most original gift which you should cherish. I would like to give you all the encouragement I can. I hope to meet you at the presentation, meanwhile you can always drop in and see me at the Thames Valley Polytechnic (if you're passing by) and have a chat. Meanwhile, keep up the writing. Yours sincerely, Violet Glasspool.

Violet sighed, remembering her own youth and the insatiable desire of the young for praise. She reached for a fresh sheet of paper.

Dear Alan, she wrote.

Violet was uncertain where her husband actually was. He had telephoned her twice since he had moved out of the flat and would not give her any clues as to his whereabouts. So far he had also refused to pay any of the housekeeping bills and a cluster of red final demand letters were mixed with the litter on the desk.

Violet Glasspool tore up the paper and began again.

Dear Alan, she wrote.

It was quite possible that he had moved in with another woman, perhaps Eva Vandriver's German au pair. He had certainly spent considerable time in the kitchen with her at Eva's last dinner party. Perhaps it was one of his students. Since they both lectured at the same polytechnic, Glasspool supposed she might have met Alan's new mistress. *It is ridiculous to carry on our conversation in this way,* she wrote sadly. *Kindly arrange for us to meet like civilised people.*

She wished that Alan would recover his toilet things from the bathroom shelf where they were marshalled like a hostile army. *It would be a kindness,* she wrote, *if you would tell me what to do with your personal belongings. Also, there are bills to be paid.*

She laid down her pen. After some thought she poured herself a small gin and tonic and inspected herself critically in the mirror. Her dress seemed suitable, she thought, if unexciting, and her hair was neat. She removed her glasses. The effect was not dramatic. Perhaps she might wear a different lipstick? The letter to Alan lay unfinished on the desk.

After she had drunk another small one, Violet put on her heavy mackintosh and left the flat. As she posted Rosemary's letter at the Underground Station, she saw a pile of magazines with bright, glossy covers from which a woman's face smiled extravagantly at the passers-by. Acting on a sudden impulse she bought a copy, exclaiming at the price. She studied the face on the cover intently, noting its white perfect teeth, the wide split of the red, shining lips, the hilarity it sought to convey. Did it bear some resemblance to Eva's au pair? Had Alan left her for a woman like this, a woman who could smile fearlessly and toss her head?

As the train rattled along the Circle Line, Violet turned over the shining pages of the magazine. On every one she was offered important advice, covering every possible kind of difficulty. 'How to rebuild your life,' she read, 'by Nina Cleverly. Yes, you can be exciting, inviting and impossible to ignore. Start here on our no-holds-barred self-inspection course. Take a good, hard look at yourself. Be honest. YES, as honest as your mum, or your man or your best friend. So you've got faults. So what! Nobody's perfect. But you CAN change youself.'

Violet was perplexed. The article made curious demands upon her. And yet, perhaps its advice could really work? She turned over more of the pages. Scientists, she read, had discovered the oil of mussels could regenerate old, tired skin. 'Old, tired skin,' Violet said aloud. 'It really works.' Here, it seemed, were the answers to her difficulties laid out in simple sentences, easy to comprehend. The reading of difficult literature, the study of science, philosophy or poetry was as nothing to the advice that oil of mussels really worked. Here was the practical advice, not vague sentiment or scolding exhortation such as she got from Alan, who told her increasingly often to pull herself together and snap out of it.

No, all this could actually be done. This was advice that could help a woman in middle life who was not looking – at this particular moment – quite her best. Eagerly Violet turned more of the pages. 'Poised to write poetry?' she read. 'Are there volumes of verse inside your head just waiting to be written? If you've a poem to pen, start here!'

With some surprise Violet studied the page more closely. She read: 'Take *Sparkle!*'s special offer of the chance to become a POET in this month's great new competition. Here's a chance to meet Gavin Jarvis, star of the unmissable TV series, "Poets in a Landscape", at this year's Coote & Balding Poetry Competition. You'll have a chance to take part in a super seminar too, where you can talk about your work and take a tip from the country's leading poets. And for the lucky winner, a weekend in Paris for two, plus a week of special tuition from Gavin Jarvis at his special poetry classes at the Porson Institute.'

So these vivacious young women were poets as well, Violet thought. Was there nothing at which they did not excel? They smiled out from the pages, dauntless all-rounders, athletes, scholars, business women, successes. Violet wondered if the *Sparkle!* competition was difficult to win. *Answer the following questions*, she read. *Remember we're looking for originality and wit:*

> i) *If you went out to dinner with Shelley would you drink*
> a) *red wine (remember he's a revolutionary)*
> b) *champagne (he's a romantic)*
> c) *sparkling water (you'd want to remember what he said to you next day!)*

Intrigued, Violet turned to the next question but the train stopped at her station and with a start she rushed out of the compartment. Clutching her copy of *Sparkle!* like a life raft she set out through the streets of Chelsea to have lunch with her former husband.

The Green Carnation was a restaurant which had been fashionable in the days when Bysouth himself had been in vogue. In those days groups of writers had gathered there to talk to each other and anyone else who would buy them a free lunch. It was the sort of place that featured constantly in the memoirs of the famous, now Bysouth's own generation, and the management proudly displayed round the walls the autographed photographs of celebrated diners in curious and already comical styles of dress.

Many of the Green Carnation's staff had stayed on while their customers, with fickle appetite, moved elsewhere, to a restaurant more fashionable, or simply stopped going out to lunch. Pluckily the ageing staff continued to serve up large portions of heavy English food to dwindling numbers of elderly customers, all the time flourishing green carnations in floral tribute at those who stepped inside.

In time the waiters grew older and the patron retired through ill-health; the aged barman became infirm. But still the Green Carnation persisted, its green paint now stained and splashed with gravy and wine, its interior even quieter. Still the same menu was served, still the chairmen of older publishing companies came to reassure themselves that despite changes in the world around them there was, even now, a stillness at the heart of things.

To Violet Glasspool, as she stood before the restaurant's gloomy threshold, it seemed that nothing had changed since the first heady day when she had lunched there with Bysouth on the day of their engagement. They had drunk champagne and conversed so loudly that even the Green Carnation's sense of propriety was offended and the head waiter had asked them to talk more quietly. Violet remembered the abandon with which Bysouth had signed a cheque for the very large bill – a cheque which later bounced and was returned by the bank to their shrill amusement. How had they managed, she wondered, to live on so little? Then she remembered that they had not managed particularly well, and that the marriage had not been a success. With a sense of defeat, Violet passed inside the gloomy entrance.

'Good morning, madam.' An old man limped towards her.

'Good morning,' said Violet, concerned to see such an elderly person attempting to hang up her coat on a hook which was proving beyond his reach. 'Do let me. Really, I can do it for myself.'

Gasping, the elderly waiter handed her a menu and

waved her to a distant table. As he leaned against the wall, fighting for breath, Violet moved between the early lunchers, noting that though hardly full, the restaurant was considerably more popular than she had expected. At least six tables were occupied. Next to her own table two elderly men were drinking water from a jug.

'A small sherry,' she said to another old man who was asking her what she wanted to drink. 'Just a tiny one.'

The waiter moved slowly away.

Bysouth was late. Violet took out her compact and stealthily inspected her face. After lunch she would definitely buy a new lipstick. So much had happened since the early days of her marriage to Bysouth. Now she was in her forties, her fifth decade. Was she a success, or a failure, or – what was perhaps worse – someone who was just unremarkable, living in an ordinary and forgettable way? How rapidly the years had gone by, like the pages of a book turned too quickly in front of her eyes, before she had properly understood their meaning.

Bysouth was absurdly late. Catching the waiter's eye she asked for another sherry. It was hours since those gins this morning, after all. How sad, she thought, to dress, such an old man in those vivid green trousers.

On the opposite side of the room she was surprised to see Walter Dove lunching with a young and very attractive girl who stared intently into his face in between mouthfuls of food. What could she see in him, Violet wondered. Dear me, he is old enough to be her father. Violet had never found Dove attractive, with his soft hands and wispy, straw-coloured hair. Why had he brought the poor girl to this dreary restaurant? Surely she would have preferred something a little livelier?

Violet became anxious. Could Bysouth have met with an accident on the way? She opened her handbag and read again the note he had sent her, inviting her to lunch. It had been a tremendous shock to hear from him again after so many years, and not wholly pleasant. The day and the time were correct. Had he perhaps forgotten issuing the invitation? Fearfully she wondered why he wanted to see her again. Perhaps it had something to do with the embarrassment of the Poetry Competition. After all these years what could they possibly have to say to each other? Would she even recognise him? If Alan was not being so cruel to her, she certainly would never have accepted the invitation. How jealous he would be when he found out she had lunched with her first husband. She caught Walter Dove's eye and waved gaily. He nodded and waved back. He, at any rate, would let Alan know about her lunch engagement, she thought happily. You could always trust Walter to gossip. Alan might even telephone to find out what she was up to.

Happily, Violet smiled to herself. 'Yes, just another small one,' she told the waiter, who was standing solicitously at her side. They must be accustomed to seeing single women stood up by their partners she thought, particularly in a place like this. The sherry was so very warming. She saw Walter Dove put his hand over the girl's slender fingers and lean forward. Nina Cleverly did not flinch but held her hand still under Dove's damp pressure.

'My dear Vi,' said Bysouth, arriving noisily. 'God bless you, my dear. What a woman! Not a day older, dear. Marvellous to see you. Marvellous.'

Flustered, Violet pressed her lips upon Bysouth's rusty cheek as he thrust it towards her. He retreated bearing the imprint of her lips.

'You're looking well, Vi,' Bysouth said loudly. Several people at nearby tables turned to stare.

'What's your secret, Vi? Can't say the same about me, can you? Don't I bloody look my age?'

He certainly did look his age. His hair, once so luxuriantly red and fiery, was matted and sparse. His cheeks were flushed and his eyes watered. Shocked, Violet smiled reassuringly.

'You look very well indeed, Desmond. It's good to see you after all this time.'

She wondered why he was calling her Vi, a name he

had never used during their brief marriage. She watched him drink a whisky at some speed.

'Well, here's to you, Vi,' said Bysouth. 'We're lasting well, but we shan't last much longer. We shall soon take our turn to ripen and rot, but for today let us live like the immortals. Today we shall disport ourselves in the Elysian Fields, with flowers at our feet and soft incense in the air. Order what you like. Push the boat out. Whatever you fancy, it's all on me.'

Violet stared into Bysouth's flushed and crimson face. It was a generous and impressive gesture.

'Have you come into money, Desmond?'

'In a way . . . I have received an unexpected windfall from a certain Poetry Competition.'

So that was why he wanted to see her. He had discovered her dreadful mistake. 'It was an unforgivable error,' she said. 'Since then I have not been able to forgive myself for not recognising your work. It was certainly some time since I last read *Bulletin from Narcissus*, but I should have had the courage of my convictions.'

'Don't trouble yourself about it, Vi,' said Bysouth. 'It was my work all right and they've had to pay me for it.'

'Pay you?'

'That's right. £5000 to cover the embarrassment. No questions asked, all expenses paid and I address the audience at the presentation ceremony.'

'I can't believe it, Desmond.'

'They are craven about the possibility of adverse publicity. Their souls are in their bellies. Well, this is one in the eye for them all. The mandarins, the professors, the kings and princes of this world are as paupers before me; after years of neglect this is my reward. All over Britain, people are reading "Memoranda to Silenus" and crying out, "Yes! that's really what a good poem should be. Who's the author? Let's have more of him. He's the man we want."'

'This must be a great encouragement for you, Desmond. Have you got any more poems for your public?

I know you were once planning a collection . . .'

'If you hadn't run away from me, Violet, you'd know I have written incessantly, every day. Not like some over-paid academic sitting in some provincial university dead from the waist down, tapping out the odd verse when he feels like it. No, I've been prolific,' said Bysouth. 'I've been writing poetry like other people make cups of tea. Up at six, every day, twenty lines before breakfast. Not all published, I admit, but that's only because of the temerity of publishers these days. They are all brain-washed by people like Gavin Jarvis; they want someone they can dress up in a velvet jacket to smile from the cover of his books. It is of no consequence to me. I write for all time, not for the men of today. There are my trans-lations too, Vi, do you remember them? The version of the *Bacchae* is nearly complete . . .'

He had started it, Violet remembered, several months before their engagement. Bysouth spoke eloquently for some time about the quality of his interpretation. She gazed at him in horror; of the man to whom she had been married there remained nothing. He was the mere husk of his former self, no more.

They ordered roast sirloin and Yorkshire pudding. Dis-creetly Violet Glasspool averted her eyes as Bysouth tried to chew his meat. 'I have been working damn hard,' he said, spitting out strands of beef as he spoke, 'so very hard this morning. I have an idea for constructing a poem – a cycle of poems – around the image of purity in our material, polluted world. Yes, what symbol could represent a kind of pristine innocence for the twentieth century? Sir Galahad? Persil washing powder? Julie Andrews? Unlikely, colliding images which I shall string together into something startling.'

'Most original,' said Violet.

'You haven't written much youself,' said Bysouth unpleasantly.

'I've published six books. Besides I'm only in my for-ties. I'm approaching the most creative period of my life.'

'You're too much of an academic to write any poetry worth reading. Stick to lecturing at your polytechnic, Vi, like your husband.'

Violet drained her glass in an attempt to dull the sting of Bysouth's words. Despite his appearance, there was, after all, a trace of his former viciousness.

'Look at Walter Dove over there,' he said, turning in his chair and waving. 'The dirty old devil!'

'The poor girl seems very young. I hope she's aware of what she's doing.'

Bysouth waved across at Dove's table in an exaggerated gesture of greeting. 'My compliments to your charming companion.'

Dove smiled coldy while Nina Cleverly accepted Bysouth's compliment unmoved.

'Good-looking girl,' Bysouth said to Violet. 'How does he do it?'

'I expect she wants to be published in his magazine,' said Violet bitterly. 'They all do. I suppose they think the sacrifice is worth it.'

Bysouth chewed noisily. 'Take Dove,' he said a few minutes later. 'What does he contribute to the world?'

'He does his job.'

'Well, you could say that we all do that, Vi. But Dove is paid considerably more than most people earn and "works", as he would put it, in the intervals between his lunch hours, savaging other people's writing. Just tell me what he contributes to life?'

'I'll tell you,' said Bysouth, answering himself. 'He's a parasite. Criticising other men's poems – lines sweated out with blood and tears – thinking of acid little sentences to ruin their reputations, amusing himself by smashing what they have created. Barren of ideas himself, Dove could spend a lifetime banging at a typewriter and never produce anything worth reading, not a single line of literature, because there is nothing inside him. He is a bag of wind, a man of straw, a eunuch. Words, words, words, Violet, mere words. That's all Dove can write, column after column, page after page.'

The wine was very cheering. Violet laughed gaily. This was just like the old days. If only Alan could see her now. Perhaps Desmond would understand how difficult it was for her to talk to Alan, to make him understand what she was really like.

'It's so difficult, isn't it, Desmond,' she began, 'to use words properly. So that other people can understand precisely what we mean by them. So often, two people can argue over quite simple ideas, because they just don't use words in quite the same way. Take love, for example. I don't think men and women mean the same thing by it all. In my own case . . .'

Bysouth's eyes assumed a glazed expression. He forced a large roast potato into his mouth.

'Take Alan and myself. We both lecture and just because my classes are sometimes better attended than his, I think he feels that I'm a threat to him. And this is such a ridiculous idea as I have told him so many times, and yet this is something which comes between us, although I'm sure that there can be a competitive element in many marriages which isn't necessarily a negative thing. Wouldn't you say so?'

'Yes.'

'I wouldn't dream of comparing Alan and myself as poets because the comparison would make no sense, and yet it's as if we're rivals, antagonistic to each other in our jobs, in our writing, in our marriage. As a matter of fact things have not been going too well between Alan and me, lately.'

'Ah.'

'I don't want to give you the wrong idea – we're not splitting up or anything like that – but it's just that there have been some difficulties.'

'Oh, yes?'

'I think part of the blame may be on my side. I have been thinking seriously about changing a little, you know becoming a little more . . . Well, changing my lipstick for instance. But I have been working very hard and Alan's last book was harshly received by the critics.'

'And your judging?' said Bysouth.

'Well, yes, the judging does take considerable time.'

'Got another?'

'Another what?'

'Another competition to judge?'

'Well, yes, as a matter of fact there's the Glastonbury Festival in a few months' time, which is an added strain, on top of all my other work. I admit I haven't been able to spend as much time in the flat as I should like to. We used to have help but it's so expensive to pay a cleaning lady these days, and I usually keep things reasonably tidy. I know Alan does like things run properly and I admit the place has become a little disorganised, but that's no reason to criticise me behind my back or indeed to confide in other people.'

'Certainly not.'

'If things are wrong, he should tell me, not Eva Vandriver's au pair. I am his wife, after all.'

'Yes. What date is the Glastonbury Festival?'

'In the spring. You see, I shall have to start all the reading for that soon. You simply can't skimp on your reading, and you've no idea of the time it takes. Alan does become quite unreasonable when I'm too busy to talk about his own work and discuss his ideas with him.'

'Shall we have a pudding?'

'A pudding? Well, no thank you, Desmond.'

'Live a little, Vi.'

'Cointreau, then,' said Violet recklessly. She felt the author of the *Sparkle!* article would have approved. Normally she never touched liqueurs. 'Be more spontaneous,' said a voice in her head. 'Be more outgoing and others will follow.'

Walter Dove leaned confidentially across the table. 'My novel is coming along quite well,' he said, 'although with *Advance* and my reviewing I just don't get enough time to work on it. But it should be finished by the spring. It's rather an outrageous, amusing sort of book. I think there are some awfully good jokes in it.'

Nina Cleverly smiled politely. Her hand was once again trapped in Dove's humid grasp.

'Perhaps you'd like to write an article for *Sparkle!* about it? It would be quite interesting, I think, for people to read about how I manage to do two jobs at once. And I could tell some amusing anecdotes.'

'That sounds very interesting.'

'Do suggest it to Madge Driller. She's such a marvellous woman, you know, Nina.' Dove's eyes were bright behind his spectacles. 'An adorable friend and an absolutely brilliant journalist, absolutely brilliant . . .'

'That poor girl,' said Violet Glasspool drunkenly. 'Look, Dove is getting quite maudlin. He's leaning all over the table. Dear me, he is almost on top of her.'

'She's a stunner,' said Bysouth with undisguised envy. 'Dove can't be a day under fifty.'

'He's younger than you are, Desmond. After all, we're none of us getting any younger.'

'Look here, Vi, have another Cointreau.' After some argument he persuaded her to take another small one. 'Shake off the dull routine,' her inner voice advised her. 'Surprise your friends by being unpredictable.'

'This poetry contest at Glastonbury –' said Bysouth.

'Yes, yes,' shouted Violet. What a bore Desmond was! 'Yes, yes, yes, another batch of boring, rotten, hopeless poems.'

'Have the entries come in?'

'Why?'

'Never mind,' said Bysouth crossly. 'Have they all come in?'

'Do you mean, is it past the closing date?'

'Yes.'

'No.'

'Good.'

'Why? What do you want to know for, Desmond?'

'I am interested for certain reasons,' said Desmond, dropping his voice. 'Just keep this to yourself will you, Vi?'

'Trust me,' said Violet, feeling her heart beginning to pound with excitement. The room spun gently and she found it hard to focus on Bysouth. She sipped her Cointreau for support.

'Suppose,' said Bysouth in a rasping whisper, 'suppose another "unknown" poem of mine were to be entered.'

'Unknown?'

'Yes. Suppose another unknown Bysouth poem were submitted anonymously.'

'Like the Coote & Balding competition.'

'Precisely.'

'But it wasn't submitted anonymously. Someone called J. W. Blanks sent it in.'

'So we are told,' said Bysouth laughing a great deal. 'J. W. Blanks himself, the reclusive poet and genius. Very good. Well, whoever sent it in, whatever name they . . . ah, selected . . . suppose my poem won again?'

Violet was troubled. 'Suppose it did?'

'Cash in the bank, no questions asked. Must be worth five hundred pounds to you at least.'

'But why should anyone send in another of your poems?' said Violet. 'whoever J. W. Blanks is, he couldn't do the same thing twice.'

'Well, perhaps he could if he needed the money. If he called himself something different.'

Violet grasped her glass. 'Do you know who Mr Blanks is, Desmond?'

'Don't worry your head about who he is, Violet. The important thing is that another Bysouth poem must win again at Glastonbury.'

'But how could it do that?'

Bysouth narrowed his eyes. 'This is where you come in, Vi.'

'Me?'

'Certainly. You are the guarantee of success.'

'Why me?'

'Because you are a judge. You could decide which of the poems should win. You could . . . fix it.'

Violet gasped in horror. 'Fix it?' she shouted. 'Fix it?' The elderly diners at the next table murmured together in the low tones of the outraged. 'How could I fix it? You're suggesting something quite monstrous, quite abominable. A travesty of my position of trust. It would be a shameful thing to do, quite unforgivable. My reputation would never recover and besides, it's quite impossible to fix something like that.'

'Bollocks!' said Bysouth rudely. 'You're a persuasive woman, Violet, you could easily influence the judgement of someone like Howard Antick, that ridiculous old man, just by the sheer force of your argument. Refusing to give in, that sort of thing.'

'I couldn't do it. Particularly not with Howard Antick. He was not impressed at all with "Memoranda to Silenus". He didn't want it to win.'

'Didn't he? Didn't he? The churlish old fool,' cried Bysouth, hitting the table. 'So he rejected my poem, did he? I shan't forget that.'

'Don't be ridiculous, Desmond. And suppose somone did send in another of your poems, what would happen if it did win? They would hardly ask you to accept another prize on behalf of some shy recluse and genius.'

'I have thought of that,' said Bysouth. 'We should need a third party. Some young scribbler who would put his own name on the poem and accept the prize in public and who, naturally would get a percentage of the profit.'

'This is quite preposterous,' said Violet Glasspool, struggling to keep the revolving room in focus. 'How could I possibly do something like that? And besides, even if another of your poems was submitted, how can you be sure that someone wouldn't recognise it as one of your early works. A judge might identify you as the author.'

With bleak honesty, Bysouth faced the truth. 'No one would recognise it, Vi. You're probably the only person who has ever read any of my stuff, and even you didn't spot "Memoranda to Silenus" as defintely my work; you only had a suspicion.'

'I did have a suspicion,' said Violet defiantly.

'A suspicion. But you didn't know for certain.'

'No, I blame myself entirely for that. I should have stood by my judgement.'

'So, what about it, Vi? You could use the money couldn't you?'

'How much?' said Violet, thinking of the unpaid bills on the desk.

'Say, ten per cent.'

'Not enough. It would have to be fifty, to make it worth my while. Even if I could contemplate doing such a terrible thing, which, as I've told you, I simply couldn't.'

'Half? That's a bit steep.'

'It is only fair. I am putting my entire reputation at risk. Take it or leave it.'

'Done,' said Bysouth hastily. 'You see, it needn't stop at just one competition. We could enter them all. At five, say, a year, we'd be talking in terms of twenty thousand, Vi.'

'I don't judge them all.'

'Well, most of them.'

'Yes, certainly most of them. Would you consider attempting second or third prize?'

'If the money was right. But I'm confident we could go for first every time, Vi.'

'Aim for the sky, not for the chimney pots,' said Violet Glasspool, waving her glass at Bysouth. 'Let's have some champagne to celebrate.' She swayed wildly on her chair, looking for one of the waiters. How *Sparkle!* would approve!

'Oh look,' said Nina Cleverly, 'that poor woman is quite drunk.'

'It's Violet Glasspool,' said Walter Dove. 'How terribly sordid. She was in a bad way when she came in, waving and grimacing at me. They've both been squinting in this direction for hours. It's terrible to see people in such a dreadful condition.'

'Who is her companion?'

'Desmond Bysouth. A frightful old man. He used to be quite famous but no one has ever heard of him now.'

'He's been staring at me for some time.'

'Ignore him,' said Dove nervously. 'We don't want him to come over.'

'A bottle of Bollinger,' Bysouth shouted, waving his arms above his head. 'We're going to make our fortune.'

Violet began to sing famous numbers from *Oklahoma* in a thin, tremulous voice.

'Have you finished, Nina,' said Dove, calling anxiously for the bill. 'I don't think we want to stay here much longer. Violet's nearly fallen off her chair. I really can't bear scenes like this. The whole restaurant is looking.'

'*I'm just a girl who can't say no,*' sang Violet.
'*I'm in a terrible fix;*
'*I always say "Come on let's go . . ."*'

'Poor things,' said Nina Cleverly as Violet fell heavily onto the floor. 'It's terrible to see such old people on a binge. It really is rather pathetic.'

7

The following day two letters were deposited in a post-box on Shaftesbury Avenue. They were both contained in long, buff envelopes and their stamps were attached in a haphazard way. Someone had typed the address imperfectly, and the wild, misaligned letters caused some trouble at the sorting office. The first letter was addressed to Howard Antick at his cottage in Epsom; the second was directed to Hubert Bacon at the head-quarters of Coote & Balding in Mayfair. The letters were removed at the seven o'clock collection and promptly delivered the next day.

When his letter arrived, Howard Antick was working in his garden. It was a cold, raw morning and the soil stuck to his boots as he bent painfully to plant some new roses. Antick's correspondence had declined in recent years. Once he had been the recipient of daily sacks of letters, sent to him by hopeful poets wondering if he might care to publish their work in his magazine. But these days he was sent very little personal correspondence. Now Antick's mail consisted largely of impersonal, printed information sheets from publishing companies or glossy brochures inviting him to invest in a set of commemorative china plates. Sometimes he would be asked to speak at a meeting of the Terpsichore Club, but Antick rarely attended these events since, inconsiderately, they did not refund his expenses. A. N. W. S. Savory had told him that they did not even pay his train fare when he travelled from Oxford to give a talk about Robert Bantam. All the same, Antick missed the excitement, remembering his younger days when he gave regular talks for the Third Programme and had been something of a name in certain circles.

Hearing the flap of his letter-box Antick hurried inside. Heedless of the thick clumps of soil which fell from his boots he saw with some disappointment the brown envelope which implied another uninteresting circular. Removing his gardening gloves, Antick took the envelope into the kitchen where he studied the address with some surprise. It was almost impossible to read, as if a maniac had been set loose upon the typewriter.

With fumbling hands Antick opened the letter.

Dear Antick, he read, *you intolerable old philistine. You may call yourself a poet, but you have never written anything worth reading in your life. How many people will remember you when you are dead (which is the real test)? You are a preposterous old phoney. Few of us will forget the talk you gave on the Third Programme in 1963 when you claimed that Robert Bantam, in his chthonic cycle Caryatids in Speluncis, was the first poet to make use of the synonymic gerund. A ludicrous assertion. Are you fit to judge poetry competitions? We think not. We think you should give up. Resign (now) or else there will be trouble. A friend.*

Antick stared at the letter. It was difficult to read since the words were composed of pieces of print cut out clumsily from a wide range of magazines and newspapers. The glue with which they had been attached to the page had obscured some of the words with a viscous film and whoever composed the letter had signed the words 'a friend' with a great flourish of purple ink which had run over half the paper. Antick held the letter up to the light, his hands trembling with the effort of keeping it straight. Then he cautiously put it down on his kitchen table and moved slowly to the cupboard where he extracted a small bottle of pills. He swallowed two. Helpless, Antick looked round the kitchen in search of immediate aid. After some moments he switched on the radio. 'Most types of cancer,' a woman's voice reassured him, 'can be treated with considerable success if the disease is diagnosed early enough. If you discover any of the following symptoms –'

Antick switched the radio off. 'Dear me,' he said, when the pills had begun to take effect, 'I have been in contact with a deranged mind. A very troubled person.' He wondered if he was under a death threat. Perhaps it was a joke from one of the poets whose work he had rejected many years ago. Perhaps it was not meant for him at all. He studied the letter again: no, quite clearly it was addressed to him. In some dismay, Antick considered the allegation about the Third Programme. The accusation was quite unfair: Bantam had been the first to use that particular technique and indeed his biographer, A. N. W. S. Savory, had committed the fact to print in his book about the poet's life. It was a matter in which he felt completely in the right. After staring at the letter again, Antick decided that he should take its contents seriously. He telephoned the police station.

Twenty minutes after Antick opened his anonymous letter, the office brought a long, buff envelope to Hubert Bacon's desk. It was marked 'Strictly Private' and Cheryl laid it on his desk with some reverence. Bacon opened the letter. He read:

You may think you have got away with it, but you haven't. You have been observed. In a certain situation, with ladies – being spanked. I know everything. I will not reveal details (of visits, etc) to your wife if you pay the sum of £200 (cash) immediately. This is cheap at the price.

Bacon began to sweat and his breath came in gasps. There were instructions on the letter about where he was to leave the money, in a Marks & Spencer carrier bag in the gentlemen's lavatory at Waterloo Station. It seemed like a practical joke, a hackneyed conceit from the worst kind of detective fiction. Surely someone was having him on.

Bacon thought about the incident that had taken place

on his way to the Banjo Club. It was inconceivable that anyone could have recognised him in that place, and yet, somebody had. Somebody had seen him and was now writing in the most horrible way, demanding money.

Thank goodness Cheryl had not opened the letter. Suppose it had been sent to his home and Doreen had discovered the truth? Bacon felt a sensation of panic. Could he dismiss the whole thing as a monstrous joke? Suppose the writer had taken photographs? Bacon buried his face in his hands. He could not afford to pay £200 just to keep a madman quiet. But what were the alternatives? The police? But that would mean a confession and he could not involve the company in his private affairs. After all, his transgression had taken place in office time. What could he possibly do? Bacon put the letter in his pocket and took two aspirins with his coffee.

Nina Cleverly opened her mail at *Sparkle!* House. One letter, written in small, sloping handwriting, was marked 'Off the record'.

Dear Ms Cleverly, she read. *Thank you for interviewing me. Obviously you have a right to say what you like about me, but do you think you could possibly leave out the fact that I left school at 16. I think it could give a bad impression in the 'literary world'. I should be very grateful. Please give my regards to Lord Broubster. Kind regards, Eddie Rosemary.*

Nina Cleverly read the letter again and then put it in her filing cabinet. 'Are you out in all weathers and still looking wonderful?' she typed. 'A great new crop of cashmere for the heart of your winter wardrobe.'

Antick was engaged in conversation with the police. 'Hello, hello?' he said, 'I am so sorry to trouble you. I have a rather annoying problem which I must disclose to you. Hello? Are you there?'

Slowly and with difficulty, since his hearing was no longer acute Antick explained his predicament to the local sergeant. 'It is a most disagreeable letter,' Antick told him repeatedly. 'It is in my opinion that action should be taken to prevent persons sending stuff like this through the post.'

The sergeant asked him if he knew the identity of his correspondent.

'I have no idea at all,' Antick shouted. 'I rather think that is for you to find out.'

The police said that they would send a man round later that day. Dissatisfied, Antick replaced the receiver. He turned again to the letter, lying like a poisonous creature that had, unnoticed, crept inside his house. Everything was still and quiet as though the arrival of the letter had somehow changed Antick's cottage irrevocably. The piles of unwashed cups leaned dangerously over the sink; the remains of his frugal breakfast – a boiled egg and toast – were stiff and cold on the table. Antick went out into his garden again but the sun had disappeared behind grey clouds and it was becoming colder. A sparrow watched him critically from the fence. Above him an aeroplane soared and disappeared into the clouds. Antick's pale blue eyes focused on the shining machine as it sped into invisibility. And so, he thought fancifully, so all my hopes go with it.

He went inside and began to compose a forceful letter to the police.

As Antick was labouring at his letter, a bulky envelope was delivered to Violet Glasspool's flat. Since she did not rise that day until lunch time it lay undiscovered on her mat for several hours. When Violet eventually emerged from her bedroom she thought, with a sudden lurch of her heart, that it might be a letter from Alan. But the writing was unfamiliar and the postmark said, 'Slough'.

Dear Miss Glasspool, she read. *Your letter meant a very great deal to me. I cannot tell you how much, in fact. It is very hard, sometimes, to work without encouragement and if the competition means that poets, real poets, people like you, see my work and like it, it will all have been worth while. It will be a great privilege for me to meet you at the poetry presentation. Meanwhile I have taken the liberty of sending you some more poems which I have written recently. No one else has seen them. Would you write and tell me what you think of them? I know it is a lot to ask, but your encouragement has meant more than you can imagine. Yours ever, Eddie Rosemary.*

A pile of poems tumbled out of the envelope written in crabbed, sloping handwriting. 'Oh dear,' said Violet. 'More poems to read. Too many poems.' She put Rosemary's manuscripts by the gas bill on her crowded desk, intending to read them soon.

The policeman who arrived to deal with Antick's correspondence was young and unsympathetic. Antick found it difficult to hear what he was saying. At one point he actually laughed at the reference to the Third Programme.

'It is not a laughing matter,' Antick told him, but the policeman simply wrote in his notebook and went away, making unsatisfactory promises.

Bacon spent the rest of the day in turmoil. At lunch time he went to his bank and stealthily withdrew £200 in five pound notes. On his way home that night, he left his carrier bag, as instructed, in the station lavatory. As he sat in his usual compartment that night, moving swiftly into the Surrey fields, it seemed to him that everything had changed. On all sides his commuting companions stared at magazines, consumed confectionery and behaved just as they always did. But the core of Bacon's life was poisoned. He faced Doreen that night with a clouded and guilty conscience and, walking round the garden for a final pipe before his Ovaltine, he re-read the letter with fascinated horror before throwing it on the dying fire and stirring its fragments into the hot ashes.

8

'Have you ever been married?' Walter Dove asked Nina
Cleverly as they came out of the cinema together. They
had been to see a particularly harrowing film of some
psychological significance to Dove since it explored
the prolonged and painful breakdown of a modern
marriage.

'I don't suppose you're old enough, are you, Nina?' he
said. 'I advise you never try it.' He paused and sighed
dramatically as they stood in the cinema entrance looking at the rain which swept down the street in heavy,
gusting bursts. The Christmas decorations which were
already in place, although there was more than a month
until the festival itself, filled him with gloomy thoughts of
family life and the long, empty days which he and Eva
would be forced to spend together, trying to talk to their
scornful, critical children.

'You see, I made a mistake and Eva can never forgive
me for it.'

'Oh dear. What was the mistake?' said Nina.

'My mistake was to marry her in the first place. She
says she was too young to know what she was doing.'

Nina half-closed her eyes as they stood waiting for a
taxi while the rain fell upon the hurrying passers-by.
How dreary it was to listen to Dove's endless complaints
about his unsuccessful marriage.

'The thing is,' he said, 'that I love women, Nina. I meet
a great many of them in my job, naturally, and I become
friendly with them. They have lovely faces, and they're
young, talented, intelligent, just like you Nina. I love all

women. I feel warm and happy when I'm with a pretty girl. I can't help it, and what's wrong with that. Why can't people be nicer to each other? Why can't we all be friendly and warm to each other whether we're married or not?'

His voice rose on a whine of self-pity.

'I believe that is a taxi,' said Nina, seeing an orange light in the distance.

Dove stepped into the road and stuck out his arm. 'Cricklewood Broadway,' he said, shuddering slightly at the address, for he had a profound dislike of the distant and unfashionable area of London where Nina occupied a small and shabby flat, an unstylish basement quite at odds with the exquisite apartments featured each month in *Sparkle!*'s interior-design pages, but the most she could afford on her singularly meagre salary. Dove's visits were rarely long, though regular.

The cab raced through the bright streets of the West End and wound its way slowly round Marble Arch. After some minutes it swung off down a congested and shabby road which led Dove away from reassuring sights and sounds. They raced out of the bright heart of London, up strange winding hills that led to the northern wastes of bed-sitters. Ninas's flat was adjacent to the railway station, a busy commuting stop and also an important loading point on the main railway line which led from St Pancras to the North. So that even when the commuters trains had made their last journey to their depots and siding sheds, the night was full of the rumblings of huge locomotives which sped past to their distant destinations.

'How far it is, darling,' said Walter Dove, watching the meter. 'It always seems that I'm leaving the world behind when I come up here. As if I'm embarking on some rash adventure.'

'Only a few minutes more,' said Nina Cleverly. 'Usually I take the bus.'

Carefully they climbed down the slippery steps which led to Nina's basement. 'I'm sorry about the smell,' she said, as they stepped into the dark sitting room. 'It comes from the dustbins. People will not wrap their rubbish properly. I have complained to the landlord.'

'They're all Rachmans at heart,' said Dove absently. He saw a row of tights hanging over the kitchen sink to dry and his heart sank. He wondered why women were always so squalid when they lived alone.

'Well, Nina, here we are,' he said, walking round the room and waving his arms. 'We have completed our adventurous journey.'

'Would you like a drink?'

'Yes, a drink, a drink,' said Dove extravagantly.

Nina poured gin into cheap glasses which were slightly smeared.

'Will water be all right?'

'Water?'

'I'm afraid I haven't any tonic.'

'Fine, just a drop of ice, darling.'

'There isn't any ice.'

'Gin and water will be lovely,' said Dove.

'Nothing but water.
And I recommend you the same prescription.'

'What?'

'Never mind,' said Dove. 'It doesn't matter.'

They sat down primly on the sofa. Dove finished his drink and there was a silence while they both tried to think of something to say. Dove looked at his watch. Then he leaned forward. Nina noted that his breath smelled of onions.

'Darling Nina,' he said and stroked her hair. 'You're looking very lovely tonight.'

Nina Cleverly put down her glass. Dove put one arm across her shoulder where it lay heavily like a dead animal.

'I've never seen you looking lovelier,' he said, stroking her cheek with the other hand. The dead hand moved from her shoulder to caress her neck while his face rubbed against hers. Dove slid from the sofa and knelt in front of her, pulling her gently towards him. Uncomfortably Nina slipped from the sofa so that they were heaped together on the floor while Dove partially removed his trousers. His legs were thin and hairy and he wore white, flapping underpants.

'This is going to be incredible,' he gasped as he lowered himself upon her. 'You're a very exciting girl, Nina.' His hands removed items of her clothing and undid fasteners.

'Darling Nina,' said Dove, moving energetically.

'Oh yes,' he shouted. 'Yes, yes, YES.'

Nina opened her eyes and saw Dove recumbent on top of her. His wispy hair had parted revealing an unsuspected baldness at the top of his head. On his neck, several inches from her face, she saw the scars of adolescent boils.

'Well,' said Dove, groping for his glasses. 'That was wonderful, Nina. Was it all right for you, darling?' In an orderly manner he replaced the garments he had discarded.

'Would you like another drink?'

Dove looked at his watch again. 'Just a quick one.'

Nina handed him another gin and water. 'I can't be too late back,' he said, straightening his tie. 'You know what Eva is like when I'm really late. God, she nags me like hell.'

'It's only ten-thirty.'

'That's bad enough,' said Dove, trying to rearrange his hair to cover the bald patch. 'It's such a damn strain at home. We're like two strangers living in the same house, never speaking to each other. I suppose we only keep up the pretence for the children, although they're out every night these days sniffing glue or getting into fights at discos. I suppose they can see through the farce all right.'

Dove finished his drink. Nina poured him another.

'It's been an exhausting day,' he said. 'That dreadful shit, Gavin Jarvis, rang me up and spent twenty minutes complaining about his payments. Frankly I don't know

112

how long I can carry on dealing with moaning contributors like him. If this job didn't drain me so much I'd have written far more by now.'

'How is your novel coming along?'

'Brilliantly,' said Dove, 'but agonisingly slowly. It's such an original, amusing theme, Nina, but I get so little time to work on it. There are all my reviews, this wretched magazine, people like Jarvis – I'm so drained in the evenings I don't do anything except drink and watch the telly.

Dove finished his gin and water. 'I'll have to go darling. I'm sorry I can't stay longer. I don't suppose I'll get a taxi at this time of night?'

'They don't often come this far out,' said Nina, 'but the Underground is still running. It isn't far to walk to the station.'

'May I ring you?'

'Yes.'

'I adore you, Nina. Do you still like your silly old Walter just a tiny bit?'

'Yes.'

'Do you want to give him another lovely kiss?'

'Yes.'

They embraced in the doorway and Dove's hand shot up her skirt. Once again she tasted onions on his tongue. Then he almost ran out through the door. After he had gone, Nina removed the empty gin glasses. Feeling hungry she went into the kitchen and looked through the almost empty shelves for something to eat. She saw a tin of soup which promised a nourishing selection of vegetables and meat – 'A Meal in a Tin' the label said. When the tin was open she saw white shreds of potato and orange vegetables floating in a greasy, yellow liquid. She ate the contents cold, straight out of the tin.

While she was eating she switched on the television.

'Next week,' Gavin Jarvis told her, 'we move to the early twentieth century and look at texts by Siegfried Sassoon and Wilfred Owen where the concept of war is authentically and relevantly problematised. Join us then.'

Gavin Jarvis smiled confidently and his face faded from the screen. There was a blast of music, in which horns and trumpets predominated the words 'Poets in a Landscape' revolved across the television set. Checking the room, in case some item of Dove's clothing – some ephemeral testimony to his visit – remained, Nina Cleverly went thoughtfully to bed where her dreams bore the imprint of Gavin Jarvis's face commenting in disapproval on the evening's ungracious union.

The next morning Nina Cleverly was working at her desk in *Sparkle!* House when Madge Driller's face suddenly appeared over the partition that separated her from the other women in the office, also crouched over their typewriters.

'You!' she said. 'This minute.'

Nina Cleverly sprang into the editor's office.

'I want to know what progress you are making on the poets.'

'Slow progress,' said Nina, 'but definite progress.'

'Is Walter Dove being helpful?'

'Very helpful.'

'He's a darling,' said Madge Driller vaguely. 'How many winners have you talked to?'

'I have interviewed one at length. The other is incommunicado.'

'Why?'

'His identity cannot be disclosed. He has an unconquerable fear of publicity. I understand he will be represented at the presentation by someone called Bysouth, who is acting on his behalf.'

Madge Driller frowned. 'Send a telegram. We want to get hold of this unknown winner. I want to find out who he is.'

'Well, that may not be possible.'

'Of course it's possible. Dove will give you a lot of help.' She started to look round the office for an effervescent tablet. 'That's all.'

'Thank you,' said Nina Cleverly. She left the room.

Dove had warned her not to interview Bysouth at any cost, explaining that he was a dangerous and undesirable person. After the scene in the Green Carnation she thought that he was probably right. Returning to her desk she began to compile her profile of Eddie Rosemary.

Over the next two weeks the weather became perceptibly colder and office workers repeatedly looked out of their windows and remarked that they expected snow any day now. Nina Cleverly completed her article about Eddie Rosemary and *Sparkle!* received a record number of entries from readers anxious to meet Gavin Jarvis and spend a week at the Porson Institute. Howard Antick and Hubert Bacon each received anonymous letter repeating the threats of the earlier correspondence. Antick immediately took his letter to the police but they said that their inquiries were proceeding and that there was nothing so far that they could do. Dissatisfied with the negligence with which his complaints were received, the elderly poet decided to approach a higher authority and wrote a letter to the Prime Minister. Eagerly he waited for a reply.

Bacon lacked Antick's spirit of combat and left another £200 at Waterloo Station. Thoughts of revelations and sudden disgrace began to oppress him and he regarded his wife daily with apprehension in case she, too, had received one of the dreadful letters. He began to sleep badly.

As Christmas approached Violet Glasspool met her former husband again, in the Dancing Cockerel, where they had a celebratory evening from which they emerged neither happy nor cheerful but miserably contemplating their lonely and mysterious Christmases. Violet laid in a generous supply of bottles to get her through the worst of it.

Eddie Rosemary found it increasingly difficult to maintain his early morning vigils in the meadows as the mornings became darker and colder. He caught influenza

115

and wrote no poetry at all as he waited with impatience for the forthcoming Coote & Balding presentation at which he would at last confront his masters.

Walter Dove completed the final chapter of his novel.

9

'We can only say,' said Hubert Bacon in a low, respectful voice, 'we can only say that without poetry we are mere vegetables, inanimate clouds of brute earth, without eyes, ears or senses.' He wondered if he had put it a little too strongly. As he drove down the almost empty motorway, his mind turned restlessly in the pursuit of a suitable metaphor with which he might introduce the Coote & Balding winners. His spirits had improved with the weather. After a dismal Christmas which was often wet and so mild that columns of midges hung suspended in mid-air in his garden, the New Year had begun with a cold brightness. No more anonymous letters arrived as the weeks went by and Bacon's thoughts turned towards the spring. Perhaps the £400 had been money well spent. Perhaps his anonymous correspondent would leave it at that.

As Bacon moved gently down the centre lane at a steady sixty miles an hour, he saw the signpost indicating the next exit to Banting. Nervously he gripped the wheel. He hoped the poets would be able to find the town, for the rail journey was complicated by changes of train. How difficult and upsetting they were to deal with. He had written nothing himself since taking on the wretched competition in the autumn. What a relief it would be to return to the genial and amusing world of *Filter Tipped*.

Banting, his destination, was once a rural village, supplying quantities of bedders and fresh vegetables to the University of Cambridge on whose outskirts it lay. But this was long ago, although the poet Robert Bantam, who would occasionally cycle to Banting in his undergraduate days, mentioned the village's 'plangent ploughs' as late as 1920 in his early autobiographical poem, 'Incompetent Georgics'. Now Banting had its own College of Higher Education and concealed its origins beneath a vigorous crop of buildings which sprang up and flourished around Coote & Balding's first cigarette factory, founded after the First World War. Although the factory caused Banting to expand beyond its natural proportions and now employed almost all its female population, the Coote & Balding management still preferred to refer to the town as rural and unspoilt.

The chairman had thought up the original and innovative idea of holding the presentation ceremony in the cigarette factory. It was, he explained, a building of architectural merit and would symbolise Coote & Balding's concern for the spiritual side of life. They had invited a specially selected group of factory workers to attend, to emphasise the company's interest in its employees' cultural attainments and the management offices had been equipped with flowers and a buffet lunch for the invited guests and celebrities. Bacon himself had raised the question of whether the factory was in practice the best site for the presentation, but the chairman argued that the Packing Hall, with its glass rooflight and classical columns, would provide a suitably aesthetic atmosphere, and besides, the boys from the local press would like the idea.

Bacon drove carefully down the High Street and turned off into the industrial estate which had multiplied around the factory grounds. It was a little after ten o'clock and the fields were white with frost in the weak sunshine. The factory stood before him, its white and green facade gleaming in the bright morning. Above the roof, a cigarette etched in white and red neon gave off a cloud of smoke which alternatively billowed and disappeared in electric repetition, creating a most effective image, especially at night. Bacon saw that a banner had

118

been draped cross the front porch, proudly proclaiming the name of Coote & Balding; a similar flag few from the roof. With a sense of swelling pride in his company, Bacon stepped across the red carpet which led to the suite of executive rooms chosen to entertain the guests. He nodded with a jocular smile to the Coote & Balding representatives who were already making preparations. They were easily identifiable by large red badges which they wore attached to their lapels; they were all smart, ferocious young men marked out for senior management and practised in company entertaining. In one corner of the boardroom a bar had been specially built and bottles of champagne were set out in a most eye-catching display. Bacon smiled with quiet satisfaction. Then he saw a familiar figure making its way towards him across the thick, beige carpet.

'Good morning, Mr, ah –' Antick extended a blue-veined hand. 'So good to see you again. What a splendid morning!'

'It's a very fine day,' said Bacon. 'You are here in good time.'

'I always like to leave early,' said Antick proudly. 'One must allow for emergencies. Many is the time I have attended this sort of function and been unpleasantly delayed by public transport. I caught the first train from Epsom and indeed it was as well that I did so since there was a considerable delay further down the line. Frozen points, I understand, hard as that is to believe. *Experientia docet*, Mr, ah. I leave plenty of time to allow for . . . all possibilites.'

'Are you the first to arrive?' said Bacon, wondering unhappily if all the poets had arrived as promptly as Antick.

'So I believe. I have seen none of the others though there is plenty of time for them to arrive. Of course,' he added, 'there is always the possibility of an accident. Gavin Jarvis will, I am sure, make his way here on his motor bicycle and there is a great risk that he may fall off. The statistics for serious injuries to riders of such

119

machines are quite appalling,' Antick said happily. 'He might easily have injured himself quite badly.'

'Oh come,' said Bacon, 'that's rather pessimistic.'

Antick smiled and said nothing. Then he leaned nearer to Bacon and breathed heavily in his face. 'There is a possibiity that I am being followed,' he said hoarsely. 'Do not look behind you, but there may be someone "tailing" me.'

Bacon looked behind Antick's shoulder but he saw no one except the cigarette executives, distinctive in their red badges. 'There are only our own Coote & Balding people. Who is following you?'

Antick put a gnarled hand to his lips. 'The Chief Inspector has promised,' he said importantly, 'to keep me under surveillance in case I am threatened with physical violence. After all, I have no idea who is writing the letters.'

Bacon's heart lurched. 'Letters?' he said. 'You are the recipient of letters?'

'Fourteen to date,' said Antick. 'A dangerously unstable person is at loose.'

'Is it blackmail?'

'I am under threat,' Antick shouted. 'The damn fool thinks I am going to resign as one of the judges, a ludicrous and erroneous supposition.'

Bacon thought of the £400 he had deposited in the gentlemen's lavatory at Waterloo. Could both he and Antick have received a letter from the same person? For a moment he experienced an almost irresistible urge to confess, to share the lonely horror of his own correspondence. And yet, was it anything more than a coincidence? They had nothing in common; they did not even share a single, mutual acquaintance. Perhaps Antick was setting a trap, trying to trick him into confession. He might even be the author of Bacon's letters himself. Bacon decided to say nothing.

'I am so sorry,' he told Antick, 'I must go through to the Packing Hall and make sure the seats have been properly arranged. My chairman will be here shortly to entertain you.'

'As you like,' said Antick. 'I'll just get myself a drink shall I? I see you have all the facilities.' He went off to the bar and Bacon saw him bear away a large glass of champagne. A sense of apprehension overwhelmed him.

Bacon went into the Packing Hall to inspect the arrangements. A raised platform had been built under the roof light and covered with red carpet. The cigarette machines had been pushed to the walls and, in the vacant space, chairs were arranged in semi-circular rows. The machines, ancient, blue metal constructions, bore towering conveyor belts along which a thousand cigarettes a minute would normally rush by. Now, although silent, they added a certain dramatic presence to the room which the press no doubt would find attractive. But Bacon wondered if they might not have done better at the local Cat and Bagpipe where the banqueting suite was said to be very comfortable.

Nevertheless the staff had done their best. Trays of cigarettes were displayed temptingly for the convenience of the guests and trailing white carnations and lilies hung from the machines. Despite their perfume, there was a strong smell of tobacco in the air.

When Eddie Rosemary woke up in Slough the day was dark and cold. He flung out his arms in his double bed, conscious of the empty space around him. Over the motorway the sky was still black, as if a brush had painted it with permanent ink. Rosemary imagined a woman beside him, a woman like Nina Cleverly, looking up slowly from the pillow, her long, golden hair spreading out like shining wires over the blue nylon sheets. Such a woman, he thought, would understand him, would read aloud to him at night and make him tea in the morning. A woman foreign to the world of Cartons (UK) Ltd, and quite unlike the women he saw every morning on the train, who sat with their knees together frowning behind spectacles or else smoking cigarettes smeared with the red grease of their lipsticks.

With a sense of exhilaration Rosemary left his bed

121

and the languorous, pleading woman and prepared himself for his coming ordeal. As he shaved he rehearsed his speech of acceptance, in which he mentioned quietly and without rancour the difficulties of writing poetry in an unpoetic age, of his own personal struggle to find an original voice. Rosemary already knew the speech by memory but, fearful of losing his concentration, he had also summarised the main points of the argument on neat cards, covered with closely written notes.

The sky was still impenetrably black as Rosemary rehearsed a fictitious private history that he had appropriated as his own, should anyone ask difficult questions about his early life. He would not, he resolved, mention his school by name unless one of the judges was persistent; in that case he would refer to a 'series' of schools. His throat was dry as he conducted imaginary conversations. He had never in his life met a poet and he wondered if they would interrogate him like dons or schoolmasters, or whether they would be vague and dreaming, or expansive with wild, staring eyes. Rosemary decided that, for himself, he would assume an air of abstract thought, that he would be unassuming yet preoccupied as a defence against the scrutiny of strangers.

With hours to spare he left the house carefully, as if he were already under inspection. His reading matter for the journey, the *Journal of Accountancy, No 16, Vol 4* and a copy of *Advance* were carefully arranged in his briefcase. His clothes, new and uncomfortable, constrained him with their unaccustomed stiffness. He had chosen a dark blue suit and a stiff white shirt, the sombre effect brightened with what he hoped was an artistic tie. With considerable shame Rosemary inserted a small instant camera (a Helsinki, on the recommendation of Lord Broubster) into the briefcase. Perhaps, in a moment of confidence, he might ask someone to photograph him: it would be important, later, to have a record.

Slough station was quiet, for the weekday commuters

changed their habits on Saturdays and became house-
bound, loitering over breakfast or strolling in gardens
where massed rhododendrons bloomed in summer and
ceramic frogs squatted by concrete pools. Rosemary
thought of his parents, crouched in front of the television
set which they would watch for the greater part of the
day. Desperately they had pleaded with him to be
allowed to come to the presentation, but with a firmness
that was savage he had forbidden them to leave their
bungalow. Buying them a giant-sized pack of Mars bars
he had induced them to stay by their fireside, promising
falsely that the ceremony would be televised. This had
convinced them and they were content to sit before the
flickering set all day, reluctant to move in case his face
should come momentarily into view and then be lost for
ever.

For Banting it was necessary to change at Paddinton
for King's Cross. Clutching his ticket, Rosemary plunged
into the darkness of the Underground to make his con-
necting journey. The impassive faces of his felllow
travellers regarded him without interest as he sat
clutching his briefcase. Suffused with his secret joy,
Rosemary sat rejoicing in his still, contained happiness.
An unsung victor he was going to his triumph.

After several stops he noticed an unaccustomed noise
at the far end of the compartment. Two middle-aged
women had moved hastily from their seats and were
coming towards him. He tried to see what had caused
their evident agitation but it was impossible to tell what
was happening. He thought he heard someone singing.

Nervously Rosemary looked away and studied the
advertisements above his head. Clearly some sort of
incident had taken place. He fervently hoped that no one
would pull the communication cord, delaying the train,
although he had allowed for such emergencies by setting off so early. The middle-aged women subsided opposite him, flushed and breathless. 'It's ridiculous,' said
one. 'I'm going to report it.'

Her friend nodded. 'It's not right, annoying people like

that. Mind you, if an inspector got on . . .'

Rosemary clutched his briefcase. The commotion came nearer. Suddenly a figure in a bowler hat came up and sat down next to him. At first Rosemary was reassured by the hat, although it was not a weekday. Then he noticed that the man was not quite right. With a start of horror Rosemary realised that he was wearing make-up. He had bright pink cheeks, blue-lidded eyes and a red, painted, glistening mouth.

'How do you do?' the man said in a loud voice. 'Be joyous.'

Crimson, Rosemary look away. Another man wearing red bathing trunks and a striped shirt with braces came up and started dancing grotesquely in front of him. A moment later he snatched Rosemary up and attempted to dance with him. 'No,' said Rosemary. 'No, please. I have an important appointment.'

The men were joined by several women dressed as rag dolls who were blowing bubbles at the other passengers. The man in the bowler hat continued to dance with Rosemary, singing as he did so:

> 'Picture you upon my knee,
> Just tea for two and two for tea . . .'

Rosemary looked for help but there was none. Abruptly he was hurled in front of the embarrassed travellers who consulted newspapers, diaries or the interior of their pockets. Rosemary opened his mouth in panic but at that moment he was thrust down into his seat again. Humbled by his shame, he looked about him for his briefcase. The man in the bowler hat bowed and as the train slowed into the station and the doors parted, he planted a lavish kiss on Rosemary's cheek. The motley company leaped and gibbered and waved goodbye to the occupants of the compartment. With relief Rosemary saw his briefcase on the floor by the doors. He lunged towards it and clutched its handle with a gasp of gratitude. But the case swung open. Papers showered out, his journal, his notebook, his memory cards. Crying out in anguish Rosemary sprang towards the doors and began to gather up the fluttering papers. As he did so the doors moved together and instantly parted again as a passenger further up the line struggled to free a plastic bag caught in the doors. In the draught caused by the pneumatic operation Rosemary's cards rose upwards in a spiralling air current and scattered down onto the electric line as the doors shut again, finally and irrevocably, and the train pulled out of the station.

Desperately Rosemary scrabbled for the cards that remained. He considered pulling the communication cord but the train was already far from the station and he had no idea how he would search the dark tunnel for the fluttering scraps of paper. Now that there was no danger of being drawn into his predicament, the other passengers were anxious to help and gathered up the impoverished contents of his briefcase. One of the middle-aged women said he ought to complain.

'You should make a statement to the authorities.'

'You want to report it,' said an elderly man. 'You want to tell them they shouldn't allow it. You wasn't doin' nothing.'

'Oh, thank you,' said Rosemary, who had now regained control of his emotions, and he gratefully received a memory card which said: 'Early life – influence of *Wuthering Heights*'.

'I believe they were actors,' said a younger man who had retrieved the copy of *Advance*. 'It's what they call "Tube Theatre". It's the latest thing.'

'It's the bloody limit,' said the old man.

'This is my stop,' said Rosemary as the train doors opened once again. Their good wishes followed him out onto the platform.

'Mind how you go, son,' said the elderly man as Rosemary walked away down the platform. For the rest of their journey the passengers discussed him with vigorous enjoyment. Miserably Rosemary boarded the train for Banting.

*   *   *

Violet Glasspool had intended to make an early start for the train but she was, as it happened, still heavily asleep as Antick strode round the Packing Hall, examining the cigarette machines with keen interest. She had spent a long and upsetting evening sorting through Alan's books, trying to remember which belonged to him and which were her own. Despite her letters to him he had only telephoned her once to say that he was never going to come back to her. She had thought it harsh to break the news in such an impersonal manner. The sorting of the books was laborious work. She had cheered herself a little by stopping for a gin every now and then, and by the end of the evening she was certainly less melancholy. Besides it was necessary to fortify herself against the affecting messages she discovered in a great many of the books: 'For Violet, my inspiration', 'For Alan, my dearest love'.

The boardroom was beginning to fill up. They had managed the catering very nicely, thought Bacon, seeing two Coote & Balding machine operators in their blue overalls handing round trays of canapés. Some people from the Arts Council had arrived and the mayor of Banting, wearing his chain, was talking to the chairman. Bacon looked round for Antick, but there was no sign of him. He had probably nipped out to the Gents, thought Bacon. It could not be wise for him to drink so much at his age.

Outside the entrance, Walter Dove and Nina Cleverly were having a conversation while the neon cigarette discharged its cloud of smoke repeatedly above them.

'Look,' said Dove, 'I may not be able to be terribly friendly to you when we get inside. I'm awfully sorry about it all.'

'Why not?'

'Well, I can't stop Eva coming to these things can I? She is a free person and as organiser of the Women's Creative Writing Study Group for the Arts Council she has been invited here in her own right.'

'You mean your wife is here?'

'Yes, she is.'

'Where?' Nina Cleverly looked across the frozen lawn.

'Well, not exactly here,' said Dove nervously. 'She has just gone off to the Ladies to do her face. But she'll be along any minute.'

'I see.'

'Look, darling, it doesn't alter anything. It's just that I won't be able to be as friendly to you as I usually am. That's all. You must just try to be very brave.'

'Yes.'

'I'd love to be able to sit next to you and introduce you to everyone, but you know my difficulties. You're looking very pretty this morning, Nina.'

'Did you come with your wife this morning?'

'We lead completely separate lives, Nina. It's a mockery of a marriage. We just don't speak to each other. I see her perhaps one evening in three – and that's only late at night when we happen to pass on the stairs. It's separate rooms, you know,' said Dove wildly. 'None of ... that sort of thing. She's even put a lock on her bedroom door. Sometimes she just leaves a note for me – "Please feed the cat".'

'Did you leave together this morning?'

'Nina, I just drove up in the car,' said Dove vaguely. 'I just drove up the motorway.'

'With your wife?'

'Bloody hell, yes, with my wife. What do you expect me to do? Leave her to come by train? Of couse she came in the car. She's hardly going to hitch-hike.'

Nina Cleverly pursed her lips and walked round to the other side of the flower bed. Dove followed her. 'When is your *Sparkle!* piece about the poets coming out?' he said, trying to placate her.

'The one you gave me so much help with?'

'Yes, that one.'

'It's in this month's magazine. We are handing out complimentary copies at the door.'

'Darling, that's marvellous,' said Dove, laying a hand on her shoulder. 'Have you got a copy for me?'

127

'No.'

'No?'

'I should think you could buy one for yourself,' said Nina Cleverly, walking off the lawn and towards the factory entrance, her high heels stabbing the icy earth.

'Oh God,' said Walter Dove, watching her disappear inside. Then he went inside too, to wait for his wife to come out of the Ladies. As he stood there, Howard Antick emerged from the Packing Hall, his tour of inspection completed. The old man gave a hoarse cry and grimaced at Dove. 'Walter, my dear chap,' he shouted. 'How are you getting on?'

'Well enough,' said Dove, walking over to him. 'Can I get you a drink, Howard? What are you having?'

'Champagne, of course.'

Dove fetched him another drink. The poet gulped it thirstily.

'Still busy at the BBC?' he said.

'The BBC?'

'Yes, you've got a programme on, haven't you?'

'No, you must be mixing me up with someone else. I haven't got a programme.'

'Yes, yes,' said Antick, with the fanatical insistence of the elderly. 'I'm sure I've seen you talking about poets. It seemed reasonably watchable.'

'No, no, you're wrong. I'm afraid. It wasn't me at all. You've confused me with Gavin Jarvis.'

'Jarvis?'

'Yes.'

'Jarvis is a damn fool,' said Antick forcefully. 'He's never written a line of poetry in his life.'

'He's very popular, I believe. He gets his picture in the bookshops and women go in to buy his poems. It puts them in the right mood, seeing his brooding eyes staring out at them. Yes, I'm afraid he is a best-seller.'

'Well, look at this,' said Antick, producing a piece of paper from his waistcoat pocket. 'Never mind young Jarvis and his motor bicycle – you see he hasn't arrived yet – what do you think of this?'

'What is it, Howard?' Dove tried to read the piece of paper which Antick was waving at him.

'It's a letter of course. Read it.'

Dove took the paper and saw that it was headed: 'From the Private Secretary of Her Majesty the Queen.'

'The Queen?' he said. 'Have you been writing to the Queen, Howard?'

'Read it, read it,' shouted the poet.

Dear Mr Antick, Dove read. *Her Majesty was very sorry to hear of your difficulties concerning the Epsom Constabulary but regrets that she is personally unable to intervene in the matter –*

'Why did you write to the Queen?' said Dove, wondering if poor old Antick had lost his senses.

'I wrote to Her Majesty to draw her attention to the appallingly low standards of police detection and investigation of serious crimes. One never knows about these things until one has first-hand experience, though over the years a number of one's friends have reported similar incidents – road blocks, invasion of liberty, intrusion into private papers. The standards are disgracefully low. It is time someone took a stand.'

'I'm sure you're right.'

'The accident rate for motor bicycles is surprisingly high, you know. I would be surprised if Jarvis turned up at all.'

Eva Vandriver came up to them. She was wearing a loose-fitting white T-shirt decorated with the sequinned outline of a tennis racquet. Underneath, the message 'New Balls Please!' appeared in large black letters. Her legs were conspicuous in bright yellow stockings intriguingly pattered with tiny Chinese idcograms.

'I might have known you'd be here,' she said to Dove. 'How many have you had?'

'Just the one,' said Dove humbly. 'You remember Mr Antick, don't you, darling?'

'Charmed,' said Antick, bowing deeply. 'It is a great pleasure to meet a lady as delightful as you and may I compliment you on your unusual and exciting stockings.'

Eva Vandriver ignored him. 'Are you going to get me a drink,' she said to Dove, 'or are you going to lean on the bar all morning?'

'Don't be cross,' said Dove ingratiatingly. 'Of course I'll get you a drink.'

'Alan Snapper is here,' she said, following him across to the bar. Unregarded, Antick bowed and nodded to her.

'Is Violet here?'

'No, no sign of Violet.' Dove heard a note of suppressed eagerness in his wife's voice.

'I wonder where she is.'

'So do I. Snapper isn't alone.'

'Good heavens. Who is he with?'

'A close friend, apparently. She's tall, blonde and has very good legs.'

'What will Violet say?'

'There's going to be the most appalling scene.'

'Particularly if Violet's had one too many.'

'Which she's had most of the time, these days.' Happily they drained their glasses. The scent of tobacco was like a drug in the air.

Most of the guests had arrived now and were studiously eating the generous quantities of peanuts and crisps supplied by the sponsors. Many sampled the free Coote & Balding cigarettes and Bacon saw Antick cramming handfuls of them into his jacket pockets. Why not, he thought, poor old man. He must be rather short these days. Ashamed to watch Antick's humiliation, he turned away.

Madge Driller came up to Bacon and waved her cigarette in his face.

'Any sign of our readers?' she shouted at him.

'What do they look like?' said Bacon.

'I have no idea. They were coming in a coach.'

'Poetry lovers all,' said Bacon in approbation.

'Barely literate,' said Madge Driller, 'judging from their entries. But we had a record number. Poetry's a sexy subject just now, God knows why, looking at all these dreadful people. Walter *darling*,' she said, waving at Dove. 'How are you my darling. I'm looking for our *Sparkle!* readers. I'm afraid the poor things have got lost on the way.'

As Dove and Madge Driller embraced warmly, Bacon looked at his watch. Still no sign of Jarvis or Violet Glasspool, or the winning poet, Eddie Rosemary. Despite the champagne he was racked by a sense of apprehension. Bacon moved towards the bar to keep an eye on the supplies, but he was waylaid by Desmond Bysouth who was drinking whisky with a companion who turned out to be the man with the wooden leg.

'Ha, ha,' shouted Bysouth, grinning at Bacon. 'Greetings. Here I am with Adrian, your old friend from the Banjo Club.'

'Hello dear,' said Adrian. 'Remember me?'

Bacon turned pale. Memories of that terrible day flooded back into his mind as he thought of the excesses of his visit to the Spanking Cinema.

'Indeed yes,' he said softly. 'How are you both?'

'Thanks for the cheque,' Bysouth shouted. Several women turned to stare at him. 'Much needed and much appreciated. I hope,' he said with intolerable meaning, 'there's more where that came from.'

Bysouth had dressed for the occasion with considerable care. His sparse hair was oiled so that it clung to the shiny surface of his scalp in lank, red shafts. He had shaved that morning and his face was red, its raw, pink surface pocked by patches of crusted blood where the razor had slipped from his uncertain grasp. He wore an old velvet jacket, a blue frilled shirt and a purple silk tie, slung negligently round his neck. He was a caricature of a poet and gave off a musty odour, which caused people to keep their distance.

'Who are all these shits?' shouted Bysouth loudly. 'The low-browed, the easily-duped, the broad-buttocked?'

Bacon lowered his voice. 'The audience has been

specially invited. There are some representatives of the local council, members of the Arts Council, the owner of the local bookshop –'

'I shall address them all,' said Bysouth. 'I shall speak with the voice of angels and tell them the truth about poetry.'

'I hope,' said Bacon, 'that your talk will not be too long. I always feel it spoils the effect, don't you think, to go on at any length. Short and sweet is the best message. Something that will catch your listener's attention and then –'

'Have no concern for my speech,' said Bysouth. 'I'm very much an expert at public speaking. Adrian, here, has often heard me talk.'

'He's done one or two things for me on the radio,' said Adrian. 'He wasn't bad, but it was rather a long time ago. Your memory probably doesn't go back that far,' he said, giggling at Bacon. 'You're an awfully reserved person, aren't you? Don't apologise, I like it. I could never stand people who gave everything away in the first five minutes.'

'Shut up, Adrian,' said Bysouth. 'Go and get us more drinks.'

'Charming, I'm sure,' said Adrian, walking stiffly across to the bar.

'Been to any good . . . cinemas, lately?' said Bysouth, shaking with some inner merriment.

'I'm so sorry,' said Bacon. 'I don't quite follow your meaning.'

'Never mind,' said Bysouth, scratching his nose. 'May all go well. There is that ludicrous old phoney, Howard Antick, boring someone to death. It is quite incredible that a senile old failure should be in charge of judging literary competitions. Do you know that everyone voted for Mr J. W. Blanks's poem except that ridiculous old man?'

'Well,' said Bacon unhappily, 'I suppose that is the reason we bothered to have judges in the first place. An interesting cross section of opinion, you see. A lively exchange of ideas.'

'He is incompetent,' said Bysouth. 'Let me tell you

something.' He put his face close to Bacon who shrank from the smell of stale alcohol and cheap after-shave lotion. 'Let me tell you that Howard Antick gave a talk on the Third Programme in 1953 in which he actually claimed that Robert Bantam pioneered –'

'Here are the drinks,' said Adrian. 'Now what are you two arguing about?'

'We're not arguing, you silly queen. Do you remember the broadcast that old charlatan gave in 1953 when he said –'

'If you would excuse me,' said Bacon, 'I must go and make sure that everyone has arrived.'

'Barbarian,' said Bysouth, watching him go. 'The barbarian in our midst. Would you get me a handful of cigarettes, Adrian?'

At the gates of the factory, the coach of *Sparkle!* poetry lovers had drawn up and was discharging its passengers. Gavin Jarvis arrived on his Kawasaki as the first *Sparkle!* reader eagerly climbed down the coach steps. She was followed by a stream of women, dressed artistically in flowered dresses and long trailing scarves. Some of them were young and many were lovely. They stared seriously at the factory gates. Most had brought notebooks in which they self-consciously made entries. some had brought cameras.

They disembarked from the coach and stood in chaste, provocative groups like nymphs in a Victorian painting. Gavin Jarvis removed his crash helmet and one of the *Sparkle!* readers pointed discreetly at him and murmured to her companions. They stared admiringly at the famous poet, approving his dark curling hair, his gleaming leather jacket and high, black leather boots. Self-consciously they moved towards him, though they were too nervous to approach directly and ask for his autograph. At last, one reader – bolder than the others – went up to him and said, 'Excuse me, is this the place where the Coote & Balding presentation is to be held?'

Jarvis waved his arm languidly. 'Through there.'

'Thank you,' said the reader. 'Actually, you're going in there too, aren't you?'

'Right,' said Jarvis.

'I thought so,' said the reader. 'Actually, you're Gavin Jarvis, aren't you?'

'Right,' said Jarvis. 'See you inside.' He picked up an armful of books from his pannier and wandered slowly down the path to the entrance porch. In silence the *Sparkle!* readers watched his narrow hips sway beneath his jacket. They followed him in silence, already overpowered by their first strange meeting.

10

On his way to the factory Gavin Jarvis had unknowingly
overtaken Eddie Rosemary on his Kawasaki. The winning poet had decided against the expense of taking a
taxi, calculating that he could claim the fare in expenses
and keep the money for himself. His new suit had been
rather too expensive. With obsessive rigour he had
rehearsed his speech throughout the train journey,
trying to forget about his memory cards now fluttering
round the tunnels of the Circle Line, or perhaps already
chewed by mice. 'Of course, I can remember every
word,' Rosemary told himself as the train sped past the
frosty fields. Earlier that morning he had been word
perfect. He stared at the pamphlets in his briefcase;
these at least remained. They would be something to fall
back on. At the station he felt his clothes were not quite
right. Did they fit him properly as the shop assistant had
promised, or were they awkward and stiff, proclaiming
his unease in an uncertain world of strangers. Eagerly
he thought of Violet Glasspool, already his benefactor,
who wanted to meet him and would be his guide in this
unknown territory.

It was raw and cold as Rosemary walked along the
road. A motor bike shot past him emitting a cloud of
foul-smelling exhaust. 'Menace,' said Rosemary.
'Maniac driver.' The factory was much further than he
had expected; at the station they had given him vague
instructions promising no more than a mile. Rosemary
began to perspire. Nervously he wondered if he had
taken the wrong road. There was no one in sight; the

road was empty and surrounded by fields apart from some horrible factories to his left. There was no one to ask. He walked on for another mile, then, as he was considering the prospect of turning back, he suddenly saw the Coote & Balding neon cigarette flashing in the sunlight.

In that instant, Rosemary's speech suddenly came into his mind, perfect, just as he had composed it, just as he had written it on his memory cards. The words unfolded in his imagination, witty, entertaining, profound. He heard the audience respond with laughter and applause as his voice rang out, perfectly judged in its timing. He saw himself bowing, acknowledging the appreciation of the crowd. There was no need to worry about anything. In spite of everything, he would carry it off brilliantly.

Boldly he stepped into the entrance porch. He gazed about him and saw red banners and women in overalls offering trays of cigarettes. As he stood in confusion one of the short-haired executives came up and shook his hand.

'I am Eddie Rosemary,' he said in a low voice.

The executive couldn't quite catch his name.

'Eddie Rosemary,' he repeated. This time his voice rang out in a shrill exclamation. 'I am one of the prizewinners, I –'

The executive shook his hand again and arranged his features into a smile. He was given a badge displaying his name which they pinned on to his suit. The executive propelled him forward into the management offices where the noise was now considerable. As he hesitated at the door, Rosemary looked round for support but his escort had gone back to the door and was already shaking someone else by the hand.

Clutching his briefcase, Rosemary stepped forward into the crowd. The odour of tobacco, mixed with the scent of the carnations, was heady. People were standing in groups, laughing and talking loudly although it was impossible to hear what they were saying. They were mostly middle-aged, he saw, and quite conventionally dressed except for a strange red-headed person in the corner who was talking to a man who seemed to have an artificial leg. Everyone was holding a drink and Coote & Balding girls walked round the room carrying trays of champagne. Rosemary stood by the wall and reached for a glass but the girl stepped deftly away from him. Everyone ignored him.

At around eleven o'clock Violet Glasspool stirred under her dishevelled bedclothes and looked in some confusion for her spectacles. Although it was now completely light, the day did not permeate through the velvet curtains which she kept permanently drawn. Violet remembered there was something important to do today, something was happening, something she must not forget. She wondered if there might be a letter from Alan and, climbing unsteadily out of bed, crept into the chilly hall to inspect the morning's mail.

There were two buff envelopes marked with the official stamps of the Gas and Electricity Boards. Clearly Alan still had not paid the bills. There was also a printed circular from *Advance*, offering three free issues if she took out a subscription now. From Alan there was nothing. Or perhaps his letter had gone astray in the post. Violet decided to ring him up.

Slowly she went to the telephone by the hall where he had written his last farewell note. Then she remembered that it was impossible for her to ring him up since he had refused to give her his telephone number, or any indication of where he was staying. 'I think I need just a little one,' she said, and moved purposefully into the kitchen where she poured herself a small, but stiff, vodka. After a few minutes the room came into focus and she saw with distaste that her slippers and dressing-gown were splashed with coffee and fragments of food.

'I'm living like a slut,' said Violet Glasspool, pouring herself another small drink. 'There's nothing like it. So much for men. It's much nicer without them.' Tears slowly began to run down her face, bringing in their wake a silted deposit of black mascara.

Violet went into the hall and peered once again at the letter-box but there was nothing inside it. She decided to attend to her make-up. Since reading the *Sparkle!* article Violet had paid particular attention to her face and her classes at the Polytechnic had been regularly surprised by the astonishing shades of lipstick she tried out on them and her rather extravagant application of eyeshadow. But what was the use of becoming a new woman, she thought sadly, when she had not seen Alan for more than three months. How ridiculous he was, running away from her like a child, believing that he would never have to see her again.

The flat was cold and empty. 'Just another little one,' said Violet Glasspool, filling up her glass. 'Here's to both my husbands. That's enough for anyone.' She sat on the bed with the bottle of vodka and a new, untried lipstick. But it was impossible to concentrate properly on her make-up since she was troubled by the sensation that there was an appointment she was urgently supposed to keep that day.

'Excuse me,' said Bacon. 'You must be our prizewinner.'

Startled, Eddie Rosemary stepped backwards as if he had been accused of committing a crime.

'Yes. Yes I am,' he said.

'Congratulations,' said Bacon, extending his hand. 'A pleasure to meet you at last, Mr Rosemary.'

'Thank you.'

'Have you had a drink?'

'No.'

'Dear me,' said Bacon. 'Let me remedy that.'

'How did you recognise me?'

'Well, I have the photograph that appeared in the paper. Although we haven't met before it was quite easy to pick you out. Your face is rather striking.'

Rosemary blushed with embarrassment. 'Is Violet Glasspool here? I particularly want to meet her. She asked me to – she has been very kind to me. Do you know what she looks like?'

'Miss Glasspool. Yes, yes, I do,' said Bacon looking worried. 'The fact is – ah. Let me introduce you to the chairman of Coote & Balding. Excuse me, Chairman, this is –'

The chairman interrupted with a noisy greeting. Rosemary offered his hand.

'If you would excuse me ...' said Bacon, melting deferentially back into the crowd. Everyone was here except Violet Glasspool. He looked round the room again but there was no sign of her. Should he telephone to make sure she had left home? Gavin Jarvis approached him.

'Hi,' he said. 'Everything under control?'

'Unfortunately I cannot locate Miss Glasspool. She doesn't seem to have arrived with any of the others.'

'She's always late for everything.'

'But if she's missed the train it's impossible that she'll now get here in time. The service is sparsely furnished, especially on Saturdays.'

'Are you sure she was coming by train?'

'Yes. We sent her a rail voucher, first class. Courtesy of the company, of course.'

'Ask her old man,' said Jarvis. 'That's Snapper over there.'

'I hardly think,' said Bacon, but Jarvis had gone up to Snapper interrupting a conversation he was having with a handsome blonde girl.

'He hasn't seen her for three months,' Jarvis shouted across the room. Tactfully Bacon moved closer.

'So sorry to trouble you,' he murmured. 'We were just wondering if by any chance you know Miss Glasspool's whereabouts?'

'Actually,' said Snapper, 'I was just talking to someone.'

The blonde girl smiled vacantly at Bacon. 'Hi,' she said. 'How are you?'

Flustered, Bacon put out his hand.

'This is Morning,' said Snapper reluctantly, 'Morning Pastime.'

'Hubert Bacon,' said Bacon. 'I'm so sorry to trouble you. I merely wondered if I might ask you for assistance.'

'They aren't together any more,' said Jarvis. 'He hasn't a clue where she is.'

Snapper looked anxiously at the blonde girl. 'No, I really don't know. I've no idea what her movements are. If she arranged to catch the train, she's almost definitely missed it, by the way, but that's just one of the difficulties of arranging anything with her. Frankly, I'm sorry, but I can't help you.'

'Who is Violet?' said Morning Pastime.

'We'll have to start without her,' said Jarvis.

'That would be most unfortunate,' said Bacon. 'We must give her a little more time.'

'If you want my opinion,' said Snapper, 'she's probably confused the presentation with some other judging in Leeds or Cornwall. I should think she's taken the wrong train to the wrong place and is now wandering about somewhere trying to find the factory. That's just the sort of bloody thing she would do.'

Bacon felt he was intruding upon private grief. 'I am so sorry.'

Jarvis struck Snapper heavily across the shoulder. 'Cheer up, mate.'

'Oh God,' said Snapper.

'Who is Violet?' said Morning Pastime.

Gavin Jarvis saw the group of *Sparkle!* readers grow animated with champagne. For their benefit he ran his hand through his hair and began to walk slowly in their direction.

Madge Driller watched him critically. 'We must get Gavin Jarvis to write for us,' she said to Nina Cleverly. 'I should think a monthly column. With a large photograph.'

'A column about poetry?' said Nina Cleverly.

'No, about women. What sort of women he likes and why.'

'Great place,' said Jarvis, passing Walter Dove.

'Yes, the architecture is terribly impressive isn't it. It was awfully inventive to hold the presentation in the factory itself, don't you think?'

'Still no cheque,' said Jarvis.

'What?' said Dove.

'Bender,' said Jarvis. 'Still no cheque.'

'Oh God,' said Dove. 'Look, I'm sorry but I've checked with our accounts department and –'

'Mr Jarvis,' said Bacon coming up to them, 'may I introduce one of our prizewinners.' He thrust Rosemary forward.

Jarvis turned round. 'Hi, how are you?'

'How do you do,' said Rosemary. There was a short silence.

'I didn't get your name,' said Jarvis.

'It's Rosemary.'

'Well, don't worry about it,' said Jarvis.

Rosemary stared at him with passionate curiosity. This was the first poet he had ever met. Having addressed him he could think of nothing to say to the exotic creature. He lowered his head and looked at his feet. He wondered if the poet would ask him a challenging question or perhaps make an observation about his work. But after some moments it became clear that the poet intended to say nothing and was in fact attempting to walk past Rosemary, continuing his interrupted passage towards the *Sparkle!* readers.

'May I say,' said Rosemary hastily, 'how much I admire your work.'

'Oh, thanks,' said Jarvis.

There was another difficult silence.

'I should really thank you,' said Rosemary, 'for reading my stuff.'

'Oh, you write, do you?' said Jarvis without enthusiasm.

'Yes,' said Rosemary, surprised. 'I write poems.'

'Great.'

Rosemary stared at Jarvis' black leather boots.

'Well, keep writing,' said Jarvis, looking round the

141

room. 'Good to meet you.' With an effort, Rosemary wrenched his eyes away from Jarvis's boots.

'I wonder if I could ask you how you yourself started to write, I mean when you first –'

'Enjoy your day,' said Jarvis. 'Look, there's someone over there I have to see. See you around.' And he sprinted swiftly across the room.

Rosemary watched him go. He stood for some minutes in the corner of the room, then he looked round for someone else to talk to.

Bacon had given way to panic. Something had undoubtedly gone wrong. Violet was still missing and the ceremony could not be delayed any longer or the guests would become unacceptably drunk. They had already cleared the plates of canapés and sandwiches, they had already emptied the bowls of crisps and peanuts. The noise of their conversation was shrill as they became exuberant. Bacon decided to telephone the railway station. Perhaps she had already arrived and was expecting to be met.

From his corner Rosemary listened to the groups of people talking to each other.

'I wondered if you knew Gareth Fardel?'

'Anyway Cardash told me he was going to Spain and offered to write a Spanish diary. I said we'd take it like a shot.'

'Do you happen to know what *a priori* means?'

'I get the impression that milk doesn't keep these days as long as it used to.'

'He's always said he was a great admirer of yours, so I assumed you were friends.'

'Anyway he filed pages of copy about castanets and donkeys.'

'I think it means "a priority", doesn't it?'

'It seems to go off after a day – even if you put it in the fridge.'

'Lots of colour stuff – blue skies, olive groves, paella . . .'

'You know, I have an *a priori* appointment at the dentist.'

'Well, he's written an incredibly unpleasant piece about you.'

'And all the time he'd been staying in Ladbroke Grove, a thousand miles from the nearest donkey.'

'You now, those horrible yellow cheesy bits.'

'Well, actually he called you a sycophantic shit.'

No one spoke to Rosemary. Friendless, he stood in solitude while the clamour of voices rang in his ears. After a few moments he fixed his eyes on a distant corner of the room and assumed an expression of deep concentration, like a man trying to solve a mathematical problem. He clutched his briefcase like a shield against the enemy.

'Glad you could make it, Howard,' said Jarvis, greeting the elderly poet.

'Of course I could make it,' said Antick. 'Naturally, I could. I must attend the presentation.'

'Violet is missing.'

'Violet Glasspool. Is she meant to be here?'

'Of course she is. She's a judge.'

'Yes, yes,' said Antick. 'I hope there is nothing . . . amiss.'

'She's lucky to miss this assembly of bourgeois complacency,' said Jarvis. 'Seen either of the winners?'

'No, I have not.'

'Neither have I.'

'They are probably among those people by the door,' said Antick indicating the group of Coote & Balding executives. 'Most unattractive young men, but what can you expect these days with comprehensive schools and no one knowing how to spell. Have you by any chance noticed someone following me?'

'No.'

'You have noticed . . . nothing?'

'No.'

'That is most interesting,' said Antick, smiling

143

mysteriously. 'It is of no consequence. Pray, don't trouble yourself about it.'

Jarvis watched him cross the room unsteadily. 'Antick is quite senile,' he said to Alan Snapper. 'He thinks that he's being followed.'

'It's amazing that they still let him out to judge these contests. I can't believe he's up to making any decision on a rational basis.'

'Rational basis?' someone shouted loudly. They saw Desmond Bysouth, his face crimson, gesturing at them. 'Antick's rational mind has long since ceased to function. He should be forcibly retired. He is old, older than you are, older than I am, as it happens. Older than any of us. His brain has not stood the test of time. He has become, to put it simply, mad:

> O, let me not be mad, not mad, sweet heaven!
> Keep me in temper: I would not be mad!

'Furthermore,' Bysouth went on, 'I can give you chapter and verse of the man's complete lunacy. Cast your minds back to the year 1953 and a certain talk on the Third Programme, when Antick announced on the air that Robert Bantam's chthonic cycle – you probably won't have heard of it, young man – contained the first example of the synonymic gerund. Now, what do you think of that?'

'No big deal,' said Jarvis, stepping away from Bysouth. 'What's your problem?'

Bysouth stared hard at him. 'Who the hell are you anyway?'

Jarvis smiled patronisingly at Bysouth. 'Forget it. You won't have heard of me.'

He was walking past Bysouth when the poet reached out a gnarled, red hand and grabbed his jacket. 'I asked you a question, sonny.'

'Fuck off,' said Jarvis.

'Look,' said Bysouth. 'I asked you a civil question. Just tell me who the hell you are so that we can all appreciate your critical judgement and then we can forget the whole thing.'

'Jesus, who is this stinking old shit?' said Jarvis loudly to Alan Snapper who retreated hastily, fearing violence.

'Look!' roared Bysouth. 'Just a simple answer to a simple question. What's your fucking name?' he hung onto Jarvis's jacket and the two poets bumped furiously against each other.

In a reluctant display of valour, Snapper attempted to get between them. 'Just leave him alone Gavin,' he said, 'he's had too much to drink. Just leave him alone and let him calm down.'

'I'm not doing anything to him,' said Jarvis. 'He started it. He's raving mad.'

By now an interested crowd had gathered round the two combatants. It was uncertain if they were actually going to fight, when Bacon, breathless and distressed, came running up to them. Stammering, he waved his arms ineffectually and said, 'Steady on chaps,' like an inept schoolmaster confronting rioting boys. Bysouth and Jarvis took no notice of him. Jarvis put his hand round Bysouth's throat and held him at arm's length, while the older poet turned purple and kicked out with his feet, trying unsuccessfully to strike at Jarvis's body.

In the moments when he was able to draw breath, Bysouth's lips repeatedly mouthed the word 'Bastards' as he jerked and danced on the end of Jarvis's arm. The confrontation might have continued for some time, with Bacon hovering uselessly and the two poets struggling with each other, if Eva Vandriver had not walked up to the fighting couple and, pausing for accurate aim, punched Gavin Jarvis hard in the left eye. 'You sod,' she hissed. 'You cheap, macho sod. Can't you see he's a pensioner.'

With a cry of pain, Jarvis let go of Bysouth and put his hands up to his injured eye. Bysouth staggered away into a distant corner, looking back in fear at Eva Vandriver as if he expected her to hit him next.

'You bloody bitch, Eva,' cried Jarvis, tenderly probing his eye. 'Christ, I could go blind.'

'Serve you right!' she shouted. 'Perhaps that would cramp your style, you bastard.'

'What are you fucking talking about?'

'You know.'

'What?'

'You bloody know.'

'Jesus, Eva.'

'Last Friday!'

'Oh God, you're not still raving about Friday?' Jarvis smoothed his hair and pushed Eva Vandriver over into a corner by the bar where they harangued each other in low, angry whispers.

In the corner, Bysouth had discovered the identity of his opponent.

'Jarvis, Jarvis,' he said. 'Of course, I might have known. The greatest con-man in the business. Have any of you read him?' he shouted at the onlookers. 'Of course you haven't. And if you had, you daren't own up.'

Bacon moved quickly over to Bysouth. 'That's quite enough.'

Bysouth's lips moved inaudibly.

'There is the matter of your speech,' said Bacon with quick inspiration.

'What do you mean?'

'It will be quite impossible, if you continue to behave like this, for you to make any speech at all. I myself shall receive the prize on behalf of J. W. Blanks and say just a few words . . .'

'Oh no you won't,' said Bysouth.

'Oh yes I will.'

'Oh no you won't.'

'Look,' said Bacon, 'don't be so childish. If you make an exhibition of yourself here we can't possibly allow you to go up on the stage and speak. We shall simply have you removed.'

'And who's going to remove me?' said Bysouth belligerently.

Bacon pointed to the front porch. 'Our executives are trained in self-defence. Any trouble and they will take you away immediately. The chairman has already authorised

146

me to remove you if necessary. The choice is yours.'

'Fascists,' said Bysouth. 'Little Hitlers. All right, yes, all right. You win. I shall conform to your petty canons of behaviour. Yes, yes, I'm perfectly all right now. I'll make the speech. Look, everyone has gone back to their drinks. All over now. Quite all right.'

'Are you sure?'

'Yes,' said Bysouth, trembling with emotion. 'Just remember there might be a few things about you the chairman would be interested to know. Just remember that.'

'What sort of things?'

'Various things,' said Bysouth mysteriously. 'Just watch your step with me. We all have our little secrets.' Bysouth pushed his way to the Gents and Bacon wondered with alarm what he might have meant. Though he did not understand the significance of Bysouth's words they remained in his mind, heavy with obscure portents of disaster.

'What was going on there?' said Madge Driller, who was drinking whisky with Walter Dove behind an arrangement of carnations.

'I'm afraid that the unsavoury Mr Bysouth has had a drop too much. He was always prone to violence. That was one of the reasons he could never hold down a steady job. One simply couldn't rely on him not to start a fight sooner or later.'

'Why was he fighting with Jarvis?'

'He has a sort of obsession about him. I'm afraid he's a highly irrational person.'

'How rarely one sees a fight these days.'

'It wasn't a real fight.'

'No.'

'Just an angry exchange.'

'Yes.'

'A heated argument.'

'I must say, I didn't know that Eva was so . . . friendly with Gavin Jarvis.'

147

'No,' said Dove rather slowly. 'No, as a matter of fact, neither did I.'

Bacon decided that they could wait no longer for Violet Glasspool to arrive. He went to the bar and banged the table with an empty bottle.

'Ladies and gentlemen,' he said. 'The presentation will take place in five minutes. Will you please take your seats in the Packing Hall.'

Reluctantly the guests moved into the large white hall, with its north-facing roof light and the decorated cigarette machines. The *Sparkle!* readers hung behind Gavin Jarvis, admiring his broad athletic shoulders and slender hips. Eddie Rosemary came on alone behind them. Confidently he ran through his speech: he was word perfect.

The smell of tobacco was almost overpowering. Above the platform the Coote & Balding banner blazed to the world and below it there was a decorated panel depicting a lyre around which various forms of creeping plants trailed. The panel, specially painted by an artistic tobacco grader, symbolised the company's commitment to art. The chairman took his seat at the centre of the stage flanked by the mayor of Banting and the leader of the Arts Council's industrial sponsorship group. Antick stepped up onto the platform which some difficulty and was led to his seat at some distance from Bysouth who also found the stairs difficult to manage. Jarvis ran nimbly up behind Bacon and sat down next to Bysouth who leered and gestured at him obscenely to the enjoyment of the audience. Violet Glasspool's empty seat was conspicuous. After a few minutes the man from the Arts Council put his briefcase on it.

The audience waited expectantly. In the front row were chairs reserved for important people like Madge Driller, Walter Dove and the owner of the Banting bookshop, who had obligingly filled his front window with a display of books by the judges in honour of the occasion. Nina Cleverly was sitting next to Adrian who

148

insisted on an aisle seat because of difficulties with his leg. As she took her seat she felt a light touch on her arm and saw Eddie Rosemary standing at her side. He laughed nervously. 'I just wondered if there was anyone sitting next to you.'

'No.'

'Could I join you?'

'Surely they will want you to sit up there on the platform?'

'Well, there isn't a chair . . .'

Nina Cleverly studied the chairs. It was true that there was no chair for Rosemary except, perhaps the vacant chair still reserved for Violet Glasspool who might in theory arrive at any moment.

'I'm sure they'll ask you to come up for your speech,' said Nina as Rosemary sat down beside her. She saw that he was perspiring.

'I was hoping I'd have a chance to meet Violet Glasspool,' he told her confidingly. 'She has given me so much encouragement, but I'm told she's isn't here. She wrote a very kind letter to me.'

'Perhaps she will arrive later.'

'I hope so,' said Rosemary. 'She said she would introduce me to lots of people.'

'Have you met everyone?'

'Not really,' said Rosemary. 'I had a brief word with Gavin Jarvis. I don't really think I really made the most of my chances with him. I'd like a moment to talk to Walter Dove after this is over. I wonder if he might consider publishing some of my work.'

'Yes. Of course, Dove is rather superficial. You might do better elsewhere.'

'I hope I was interesting enough for your article,' said Rosemary. 'When is it coming out?'

'It's published in the current issue. There are copies here.'

'Here?' said Rosemary, in intense excitement.

'Yes, a *Sparkle!* girl is handing them out. I'm surprised you weren't given one.'

'Yes. How curious it will be to read about myself,' said Rosemary, twisting his hands together. 'To see yourself through the eyes of someone else – a complete stranger who comes into your house and decides what you're like in a couple of hours. And a photograph, too.'

'Yes, I think you'll like the picture. It makes you look very striking.'

'Perhaps I should get more than one copy.'

'You might like to give some to your friends.'

'I suppose I should read the article first . . .'

Bacon stood up on the platform and introduced the chairman. There was a burst of polite applause. The chairman rose slowly and leaned forward. The audience sank back into their chairs and began to study their unusual surroundings.

The chairman spoke softly in a low, cultivated voice. He mentioned the importance of art in the world of commerce, emphasised the value of poets who, while they did not actually produce anything, nevertheless enriched the quality of daily life by improving the nation's leisure hours. He praised the benefits of self-expression for all, he compared life without poetry to a machine without oil, its cogs inefficient and rusty without the embrocation of verse. He pointed out that poetry had sustained many through periods of doubt and depression. He spoke at length of his own experiences during the Second World War when he had withstood the difficulties of imprisonment in a German prison camp by recalling passages of Tennyson he had been required to learn by heart at school:

> *I will not die alone, for fiery thoughts*
> *Do shape themselves within me, more and more,*
> *Whereof I catch the issue, as I hear*
> *Dead sounds at night come from the inmost hills,*
> *Like footsteps upon wool . . .'*

declared the chairman obscurely. The audience sighed and rustled, shifting on their seats like leaves on a windy day.

On the platform it was clear that Antick was experiencing difficulty in hearing what was being said. At intervals he would lean towards the chairman and say, 'Eh?' or 'Speak up a bit'. In turn Bysouth would whisper loudly at him to be quiet. 'Shut up you silly old man,' he hissed as Antick loudly called out, 'Can't hear up at the front, sir.' Fortunately the elderly poet did not hear Bysouth's remarks.

The chairman moved on to a wider sphere. He spoke of the value of poetry in the world of politics, giving our leaders glimpses of more permanent values than the ephemeral preoccupations of petty legislation. He spoke of the part of the mind that guides the judgement; of his own reliance on the words of the great writers when making decisions. He said, earnestly, that poetry must be supported by more than sentiment alone, and praised the enlightenment of those industries who gave financial support to artistic enterprises like the poetry competition. Coote & Balding money, he declared proudly, would pay for a new generation of poets, the rebirth of enthusiasm and inspiration for a new age. It would enable people like – and here he dived uneasily for his notes until Bacon audibly prompted him – people like Eddie Rosemary and J. W. Blanks to carry on their craft just as in the days of the Renaissance poets prospered and flourished at the courts of the bankers, the industrialists, the men of business.

'Lastly,' said the chairman, 'let us not overlook the enormous contribution to the success of this day made by Mr Hubert Bacon, who has arranged that everything should run so smoothly and effortlessly and indeed perhaps we show our gratitude to him most by forgetting that he is here, pulling the strings and turning the cogs in our midst.'

There was a ripple of applause. Bacon rose to acknowledge the tribute to his services. Several people (all Coote & Balding employees) shouted, 'Jolly good' or 'Well done'. Bacon lowered his head modestly.

'It was nothing,' he told them softly. 'Nothing at all.

No, indeed. Very kind, thank you so much.'

With a satisfied expression Bacon sat down. The chairman tapped him on the shoulder and he sprang once more to his feet. 'The next stage of the ceremony will now take place,' he said. 'As you may know, Coote & Balding is proud to present a cheque for £5000 to each of our two winners who have been chosen by a distinguished panel of poets. With this money we hope we may play our part in encouraging them to go forward and devote themselves to their art spared, perhaps, from some of the financial worry which might otherwise have prevented them from developing their powers to the heights of which they are capable.'

Sympathetically the audience applauded. Bacon looked at Violet's empty chair. 'Unfortunately one of our number is sadly absent. Miss Violet Glasspool, a distinguished lady poetess who was to have been with us this afternoon, has been unavoidably detained. She sends her sincere apologies and, I know, would like me to say at this point how much she is thinking of us all here this afternoon.'

Once again the audience clapped. Eddie Rosemary swallowed nervously.

'We are also privileged,' said Bacon, 'to have with us Mr Howard Antick, a noted poet –'

'Bollocks!' shouted Bysouth.

'– and a distinguished literary critic. And last, but not least, our third judge is Mr Gavin Jarvis who is, I am sure, a familiar face from his highly successful television programme, "Poets in a Landscape". The judges will shortly tell us how they made their decisions, but first I must ask our prizewinners to come and receive their cheques from the chairman of Coote & Balding.'

Faint with anxiety Rosemary got to his feet and looked blindly for the stairs. Slowly he moved towards them, and began to climb up towards the exalted ranks of dignitaries.

'Unfortunately,' said Bacon, 'Mr J. W. Blanks cannot be here in person to receive his prize. He suffers from a rare psychological complaint which renders him unable to countenance publicity. On his behalf, Mr Desmond Bysouth, a close friend and noted poet, will receive the prize.'

Bysouth also rose to his feet and he and Rosemary presented themselves to the chairman at exactly the same moment.

'Move over,' said Bysouth, pushing in front of Rosemary.

'Congratulations. Very well done, Mr Rosemary,' said the chairman, giving a cheque to Bysouth.

Bysouth turned and made a grab for the microphone but Bacon interposed himself between the instrument and the poet. 'You're not going first,' he whispered as the chairman said, 'Splendid effort, a great achievement, Mr Blanks,' to Eddie Rosemary. A Coote & Balding photographer, crouching at the foot of the platform, illuminated them all suddenly in a flash of blinding light. 'You go first,' said Bacon, pushing Rosemary towards the microphone. He said to the audience: 'Ladies and gentlemen, Mr Eddie Rosemary.'

There was more applause. The lights of the camera flashed again. Blinking, Rosemary stared out at the pleasant, smiling faces lifted toward him.

'Ladies and gentlemen,' he said, his voice rasping in his throat, 'It is, it is . . . a very great honour to, to . . .'

If only he had his cards. His hands fumbled for them, missing their rectangular solidity.

'I never dreamed that I . . . it is something that I have, er, have worked for for so long, so long, unworthy as I am . . .'

With horror he heard his own words spilling out in incomprehensible gibberish, confusing and unaccountable to everyone there. He gazed at them as they stared with kindly, distressed faces. What had he planned to say? What were his themes? Wordsworth? Keats? 'It is Keats whom I should thank for his . . .'

If only his cards were there. If only he could have held on to something. He saw Bacon rise and clear his throat.

153

Desperately he continued, 'This moment of recognition, something that will live, a theme for song, as Homer said . . .'

'Thank you so much,' said Bacon firmly. 'Congratulations once again on your prize.'

Stumbling, Eddie Rosemary left the platform, his mouth dry, his eyes burning. He hardly saw the clapping hands, the faces which nodded and smiled. He could not find his seat and went out through a door marked 'Authorised personel only', trying to escape them all. No one followed him. He found himself in a room which was entirely full of raw tobacco, lying in large bales round the walls. He could hear Bacon's voice rising and falling in the Packing Hall announcing Bysouth. Once again he heard the swelling applause, in such a way they had clapped for him. In misery he shredded the moist tobacco between his fingers. It was all going ahead, they were carrying on without him. The moment was past. If only he had not lost his cards he could have told them exactly what he meant to say.

Suddenly the speech came back quite clearly into his mind, his brilliant speech, just as he had written it. He could remember it all. It was simply the unexpected sea of faces which had caused him momentarily to falter, all those flashing lights and all that applause. The paragraphs sprang to life before his eyes. He could do it now. He would go back and murmur something to Bacon and they would let him make a speech again before the discussion was opened to the floor. Sweating, Rosemary leaped up from his tobacco bale and pushed open the door. He could clearly hear Bacon introducing Bysouth. He ran along a corridor and pushed open another door. This time he entered a room filled with bales of white lint which, unknown to him, was eventually to be compressed into the famous Coote & Balding Kleen 'n Klear special filter. There were two doors. In panic he pushed open the one which seemed nearest to the sound of Bacon's steadily rising and falling voice. He ran down a long corridor.

'On behalf of our second winner,' said Bacon, 'Mr Bysouth will say just a few words.'

Bysouth moved towards the microphone and jerked it towards him as if pulling a turnip from the ground.

'The politicians, the businessmen, the bankers of the world shall not betray us,' he shouted at the audience. 'Let the poets speak the truth, let them speak of our age and for our imagination. Who reads poetry now?' Shocked by the loudness of Bysouth's voice, several people turned and laughed nervously to their neighbours. 'Do you? Do you?' the poet shouted, pointing his finger at individuals in the crowd. 'Do you?' His eye came to rest on the *Sparkle!* reader who had approached Gavin Jarvis in the car park. Fortunately she was used to this direct method of approach since she was a member of the London Dental Nurses Group and attended a regular creative workshop for all dental nurses who wanted to develop their writing skills.

'Yes, certainly,' she shouted back. 'Emily Dickinson, Sylvia Plath and . . . Gavin Jarvis.' She gazed hopefully at Jarvis as he sat making occasional notes on the platform but he gave no acknowledgement of her literary tribute. Bysouth was taken aback. He ignored her and changed his theme.

'Poetry is like the sea,' he said. 'It is the blood and bones of the world, the stones and the sand. It is from age to age. And none of you have any idea of what it is to be a poet as you sit here with your drinks and sandwiches and free cigarettes.'

The audience listened with enjoyment. Here, at last, was the kind of speech they had come to hear. Poets, they knew, were wild and eccentric by nature. Here was something like the authentic poet, with his strange red hair and angry, rasping voice.

'I am here to accept the cheque,' said Bysouth, 'on behalf of a writer who cannot be here today, J. W. Blanks. It is a great pity you are denied the chance of meeting him, but he is of a shy and retiring disposition. Yes, he is a shrinking violet. He is a modest, quiet and intensely brilliant man. His ... thoughts, I know, are with us all this afternoon.' There was a short pause as Bysouth appeared to double up with mysterious laughter. 'Yes,' he said, 'Mr Blanks is still unknown, but posterity will come to know him. You are fortunate to have heard his work today. I shall now read the winning poem, "Memoranda to Silenus".'

Running along the dim corridor, Rosemary heard Bysouth's voice declaiming the obscure lines of his poem. He had not read "Beyond the Zebra Crossing" to them; they had not given him a chance. In fear and anguish of spirit he plunged through another door into a room full of switches and levers. Weeping openly now he stopped for breath, completely lost in this brutish, hostile place. How could he get out? How could he get back to the Packing Hall and read his poem? He opened another door in despair but it only led into the same bewildering corridor again. Labyrinthine, the walls closed about him.

Bysouth finished the poem in a triumphant climax. Then he laid down the paper.

'There are some people who have strange ideas about poetry. There are those who would heap chains on Prometheus, who would bind him to the rock with the help of an Arts Council grant. Relentless ambition drives men forward beyond the limits of their grey and bucolic brains; they are impaled upon the inaccuracies of their utterances. For example there are those among us today who should be cast out from this hall; those who actually observed in 1953, during a talk on the Third Programme, that Robert Bantam was the first writer ever to make use of the principle of the synonymic gerund. Yes. Ha! I thought that would stun you.'

The audience looked on, baffled and comfortable. This was what they expected to hear from a poet; none of them attempted to understand. On the platform Antick nodded vigorously and began to make copious notes on the back of his programme. His scaly tongue protruded as he wrote with concentration.

'There are those who claim to be poets who appear on television, who have never written poetry in their lives, who have surrendered to the principle of making money at the expense of art.' His face turned red and he began to speak more quickly. 'And yet we make them judges. We sit at their right hands and scramble for the crumbs they offer us. *Quis custodiet ipsos custodes*? Sexual pleasure is the only true reality; all other activities are an unsatisfactory substitute.'

By now he had completely lost the audience. Bysouth leaned towards them. 'You are scum,' he said distinctly. 'The unwholesome multitude, the self-righteous bourgeoisie, congratulating yourselves on your tawdry competitions, your worthy participation in culture. I could write better poems than any of you with a pen stuck up my arse. I have contempt for you all, puffed up, ignorant fragments of chaff. I think you're a lot of farts.

Bysouth suddenly subsided onto his chair. He was breathing heavily and his face was purple. Adrian turned to Nina Cleverly: 'I told you he was a marvellous public speaker.'

'A rather controversial speech,' said Nina Cleverly. 'I had expected something more conventional.'

'They really enjoyed it,' said Adrian. And indeed the audience were clapping with marked enthusiasm as Bysouth gasped for breath. 'No one's understood a word of it,' he said, 'except for that rude bit at the end, and they all expect poets to talk like that.'

The Coote & Balding chairman and the man from the Arts Council nodded at each other and smiled. Bacon rose to his feet.

'Thank you so much, Mr Bysouth,' he said, 'for that challenging and refreshing speech which has certainly given us all something to think about I'm sure. I hope we shall all be stimulated to contribute to the discussion which will now follow.' The audience once again broke into enthusiastic applause.

'And now,' said Bacon. 'I shall open up proceedings to the floor. Are there any questions you would like to ask? Perhaps Mr Rosemary would like to come up and join us on the platform?' There was no movement in the audience. 'Mr Rosemary?' Bacon repeated. There was no response. 'Is he perhaps no longer with us?'

Lost in the blackness of his prison, Eddie Rosemary dried his tears and, giving way to the desperate promptings of panic, grasped two of the red levers and pulled them forcefully. With luck they might activate the alarm system and lead to his discovery. He waited for the sound of bells or the clamour of voices. But in his sequestered cell he heard nothing. In the Packing Hall the ceremony was dramatically interrupted.

As Bacon waited awkwardly for someone to volunteer a question there was suddenly a tremendous rattle of machinery. With one accord the nine cigarette machines which lined the walls burst into thunderous activity and began their daily labour of producing cigarettes. The noise was considerable as the shuddering conveyor belts began to revolve, gathering speed and throwing off their garlands of flowers.

A thousand cigarettes spilled over the floor as the shining machines emitted perfect examples of the company's special Extra-Long Menthol Luxury Kings. There was panic in the audience; women screamed and struck their neighbours in the rush to get to the exit doors. Men pushed them aside, running along the rows of chairs, striking down impediments in their way. The Coote & Balding executives attempted to reach the thundering machines but in the confusion it was impossible for them to make their way through the crowd. Gavin Jarvis jumped from the platform and ran to the nearest exit, colliding with Madge Driller and pushing her over as she attempted to marshal the *Sparkle!* readers.

'The machines have taken over,' cried Bysouth in alarm and he rushed from the platform, pushing against

Antick's chair as he did so and sending the elderly poet flying from his seat into the panicking audience where he disappeared under stamping feet. He fell heavily with a cry of terror and lay on the floor without moving.

'Ambulance! Police!' screamed Bacon, completely losing his head. 'Somebody has been killed. This is an emergency.'

The chairman rushed past him, fighting his way through the screaming crowd to the machines. Then, as suddenly as they had burst into life, the glittering blue engines were silent; the chairman had switched them off. The remnants of the audience, scattered at the far corners of the hall, fell silent too, calmed by the sudden peace. The chairman climbed onto one of the machines.

'There is no need to panic,' he said. 'No one has been hurt. Please leave in an orderly manner through the exit doors which are clearly marked.'

Nina Cleverly held Adrian's hand for moral support. 'Who switched the machines on?'

'It's a miracle no one was killed. Or have they been?' Adrian pointed to the figure of Antick lying motionless on the floor. A small crowd gathered round him.

'Is he dead?' said Madge Driller. 'You must give him the kiss of life.'

'Is there a doctor here?' shouted Bacon.

But after some minutes it became clear that their fears were groundless for Antick was seen to open his eyes and slowly to assume an expression of agitation.

'He's getting up,' said Madge Driller. 'Where are all my girls?' Out in the car park Jarvis was offering a lift on his motor bike to one of the *Sparkle!* readers.

'How very unfortunate,' said Walter Dove, hurrying over to them. 'Everyone is leaving. A most upsetting experience.'

'Are you all right, Mr Antick?' said Bacon.

One of the Coote & Balding girls came over with a First Aid pack.

'He seems to be okay,' said Adrian.

'They are giving him a cup of tea,' said Nina Cleverly.

'He is trying to talk.'

'He's started shouting.'

'At his age anything could happen. His heart could simply stop.'

'Poor love. Let's hope he hangs on.'

'I'm afraid Mr Antick is unwell,' said Madge Driller solicitously holding his tea cup.

'Nonsense,' said Antick. 'Perfectly all right now. I can categorically state that I have been given an important clue this afternoon and I am now in an authoritative position to make a statement to the police. Please call me a constable. There is one detailed to follow me. Please call him out.'

'Poor Mr Antick is suffering from shock,' said Madge Driller.

'It is a police matter,' said Antick. 'Just give him a call would you? Constable! Constable!'

'Walter, darling,' said Madge Driller, 'would you be able to drive poor Mr Antick home?'

'Where?' said Dove, looking at Nina Cleverly.

'Where do you live, Mr Antick?'

'He lives in Epsom,' said Bacon. 'I have corresponded with him there.'

'I insist on making a statement,' Antick shouted at them. 'Just let me get up and speak to the constable.'

'Are you sure we shouldn't call a doctor?' said Dove.

'An ambulance would finish him off. He will be perfectly all right if you would drive him home,' said Madge Driller.

Dove looked at Nina Cleverly again. 'Actually I wasn't going straight home,' he said. 'Anyway, it's very difficult to get to Antick's cottage. I went there once, but I don't suppose I could find it now. It's in the country somewhere. He has rather a nice garden.'

'What is your address, Mr Antick?' said Madge Driller.

'What's that? Speak up, would you?'

'What is your address?' she shouted, bending down and breathing a cloud of cigarette smoke in his face.

'I have no intention of going home,' said Antick, sensing an attempt to dispose of him.

'We think it would be best,' said Bacon.

'Much the wisest course,' said Madge Driller.

'Madam, I think not,' said Antick.

'Wouldn't you like to put your feet up quietly at home?'

'Thank you, but I should not like that at all.'

'Someone must look after him,' said Bacon. 'The chairman would be most upset if we simply left him alone.'

'There is nothing the matter with me at all,' said Antick, getting up out of his chair. He swayed alarmingly and Dove rushed over to support him. 'If you would be good enough to call me a taxi,' said Antick, 'I shall be quite all right. Quite all right, thank you.'

'He wants a taxi.'

'If Walter wasn't so selfish,' said Madge Driller, 'he could drive him home quite safely and deliver him to the doorstep.'

'I'm not leaving yet,' said Dove. 'I have a business appointment.'

Bacon began to apologise profusely to Antick and asked if there was anything the company could do.

'Just a taxi, if you would be so kind,' said Antick. 'There is nothing wrong with me at all.'

Bacon went away to call the taxi.

'After all,' said Dove, 'we can't actually tell him what to do. He isn't our responsibility.'

'He seems to know what he's doing,' said Madge Driller. 'I suppose we must let him do what he wants.'

'Howard are you sure you're all right?' said Dove. 'Feeling a bit queasy, are you? Just put your head between your knees and you'll be fine.'

With some concern they watched Antick labouring for breath. Dove climbed onto the stage and seized a piece of paper on which Bysouth had made the notes for his baffling speech. He fanned the gasping poet vigorously. After some moments Antick's face lost its grey pallor.

'I must take a couple of my pills,' he said, delving into his jacket pocket. 'Just one moment while I –'

'Get him some water,' said Madge Driller. 'He wants to take some pills.'

'He's got a cup of tea.'

'He wants some water too.'

'What are they for, Howard?' said Dove anxiously. 'Heart? I've got some rather the same colour. Mine are for blood.'

'Never mind that,' said Madge Driller. 'Who cares about your blood, Walter? Mr Antick is in distress.'

They brought him water and Antick took the pills. 'Thank you,' he said, fanning himself with Bysouth's speech. 'No need to worry, perfectly all right now. Most grateful for . . .' Suddenly Antick was silent. He stared at the sheet of paper which was covered with purple handwriting and smoothed it out on his knee. After he had studied it intently he smiled and said, 'Ah yes, yes, yes. Indeed. Just as I thought.'

'Do come and lie down,' said Madge Driller.

'This is incontrovertible proof,' said Antick. 'No doubt about it at all. My suspicions are entirely confirmed. As I said, the police will know precisely what to do.'

Bacon came back. 'The taxi is waiting.'

'So kind,' said Antick, absently pressing some silver into his hand. They guided him to the front porch and watched him leave in the taxi.

'In my opinion,' said Madge Driller, 'that old man is suffering from some temporary derangement.'

Dove laughed in a knowing way. 'Nothing unusual in that. In fact, he's not really fit for this sort of thing you know. These competitions get rather too much for him. Of course, he likes to be involved and everyone humours him but things have changed rather since his day.'

'Poor old chap,' said Bacon. 'One fears that this will be his last competition. One must hope he has not hurt himself too badly. I'm not certain of the company's position on an insurance claim . . .'

Dove looked for Nina Cleverly and found her in the car

park with Adrian and Bysouth, who had emerged from behind the *Sparkle!* coach where he had been taking cover. Then he saw Eva Vandriver coming towards him.

'Where were you?' she said scornfully. 'I was knocked over by some overweight chauvinist who runs the local bookshop.'

'It has been a disaster.'

'A farce. Where is Jarvis, do you happen to know?'

'Jarvis?'

'Yes. Don't be such a fool, Walter. Did you see him leave?'

'I didn't notice.'

'Oh, bloody hell!'

'I'm sorry, Eva.'

Madge Driller came up to them. 'One of the *Sparkle!* readers is missing,' she said. 'I don't suppose either of you has seen her?'

In reply Eva Vandriver turned angrily away.

'She's looking for Gavin Jarvis,' said Dove.

'He's gone too,' said Madge Driller.

Rosemary crouched trembling in the tiny room for several minutes but nothing happened. No one came. After some time he opened one of the doors and looked down the long corridor. He ran down its entire length and plunged through another door marked 'Emergency Exit Only'. To his surprise he found himself out in the fresh air, facing a collection of outhouses in rough red brick and several large industrial dustbins. There was no sign of the Coote & Balding banners or the neon cigarette. He must have come out at the back entrance. The wind was icy and there were light but persistent flakes of snow in the bitter air. Rosemary's tears were over. They dried stale on his cheeks as the sun grew pale behind the brick buildings and the sky darkened with the approaching night. He thought of the audience discussing the winning poems without him and of his failure on the platform. He decided to leave the scene of his defeat, to escape the contemptuous and unforgiving stares of the audience.

He ran quickly through the outhouses and down a long, broad path which led to a main road. It was, he discovered, the same road along which he had walked with such buoyant expectations three hours ago. He began to walk quickly towards the distant outline of the office blocks that signalled the heart of Banting.

'Nina, Nina, I just wanted –' Walter Dove grasped Nina Cleverly's elbow as she stood in the car park with Adrian and Bysouth. He had been running after her and was out of breath.'

'Did you want something?'

'I wondered if I might give you a lift?'

'I have one already. Mr Bysouth has kindly offered to run me back to town.'

Dove looked in dismay at Bysouth and his companion.

'Will Antick be all right?' asked Nina Cleverly. 'We were worried about his accident.'

'We just don't know,' said Dove, speaking in a quiet, reverent voice as if Antick was already dead. 'I wondered if I could take you out for a drink, then we could have some dinner.' He was acutely conscious of Bysouth staring at him with undisguised interest.

'Would you like that, Nina? Will you have dinner with me?'

'No.'

Dove stared at her imploringly. 'Eva is making her own way home. Would you like me to drive you back to London?'

'Not very much.'

'Perhaps you'd like to go for a walk in the country and we could find a little country pub . . .'

'Frankly,' said Nina Cleverly, 'I don't want to spend an evening with you at all.'

'You don't?'

'No.'

'Oh dear,' said Dove. 'That's very disappointing for me darling. Couldn't we talk about this somewhere?'

'No.'

'Look, if you feel like this, shall I ring you up later at home?'

'No.'

'Well, when shall I ring you up?'

'I'd rather you didn't ring me up at all.'

'What, never?'

'Yes.'

'Why. What's the matter?'

'I don't want to discuss it.'

'I feel very upset,' said Dove.

'You have my sympathy,' said Bysouth, a keen spectator.

'Oh God, what's wrong with my life?' said Dove.

'You're talking like a bad novel,' said Nina Cleverly. 'I really must go.'

Dove watched her and Adrian climb uncomfortably into Bysouth's sports car in which they left the park at an unsuitably high speed.

'Coming for a bevvy?' said Alan Snapper, passing Dove with Morning Pastime.

'My God, I just don't understand women at all,' said Dove.

'Where's Eva?'

'It's not Eva who's the problem'

'Oh I see,' said Snapper. 'What a ghastly afternoon.'

'Do they know who turned the machines on?'

'No. They think it must have been an electrical fault.'

'Well, I'll come and have a drink with you,' said Dove. 'I feel absolutely drained, my nerves are –' He stopped and looked in some agitation round the car park.

'What's up?' said Snapper.

'She's taken the car,' said Dove. 'Eva's gone off in the car to look for Jarvis. What a cow!'

'We can give you a lift,' said Snapper. 'We came in Morning's car.'

'Thanks,' said Dove. 'You know, I can't understand how a woman can be perfectly rational and charming at one moment and then act in an unbalanced, lunatic way the next. I just don't think it's normal.'

165

'Women aren't,' said Snapper, slapping Morning Pastime hard on her buttocks. She smiled, and giggled at him.

'Of course,' said Dove, following them to the car, 'my life with Eva has exposed me, in a way, to the irrational side of women's behaviour. She blames me for everything that has gone wrong with her life, she says I've spoiled any chance she ever had of being a person in her own right. Everything's my fault, everything's wrong because of me . . .' Dove talked on as they drove out of the car park to find a drink in Banting.

11

Sitting in the back of his taxi Antick felt his sensation of giddiness gradually recede. The world, rather than spinning rapidly around him, steadied and slowed down. The taxi driver swung right at the large round-about in the centre of Banting and Antick saw signs indicating that they were about to approach the motor-way leading back to London. Suspiciously he tapped the driver lightly on the shoulder.

'There seems to be some confusion. We are not going in the direction I have requested.'

The taxi driver took no notice and continued to drive along the road.

Antick rapped him lightly on the shoulder with his walking stick.

'I fear we are not going in the right direction.'

'Mind that stick,' said the driver. 'You could do some-one an injury with that.'

'Let us hope,' said Antick, 'that it will not come to that. Meanwhile, as I say, you are going in the wrong direction.'

'They said you wanted to go to Epsom,' said the driver. 'That's what the gent who booked me said.'

'But that is not where I want to go.'

The taxi driver hesitated. He had been given instructions by Bacon to take the elderly party back home since he had been knocked on the head and was not in full possession of his senses. He decided to con-tinue driving in the direction of the motorway.

As the car sped on, accelerating slightly, Antick

noticed another signpost declaring that the motorway was only a hundred yards ahead. He knocked the driver on the shoulder with his stick, this time employing considerable force.

'Leave off, squire,' said the driver. 'Do us a favour.'

'I am sorry to trouble you,' said Antick, 'but I simply do not want to go to Epsom. Would you be kind enough to turn the car round and conduct me to the nearest police station.'

'Police?'

'Yes please,' said Antick with determination. 'Unless you intend to kidnap me – an offence punishable by imprisonment – you must be good enough to carry out my wishes. Otherwise –' and Antick's voice rose in agitation, '– otherwise I may be forced, in defence of my person, to strike you rather hard with my stick.'

The taxi driver looked into his rear mirror and observed that Antick's blue, roughened fingers were coiled round his walking stick. The old man's eyes, though watering profusely, were nevertheless bright and resolute.

'It's more than my job's worth . . .' the taxi driver said, remembering Bacon's large tip, but Antick cried, 'The police station immediately,' and the driver gave in. 'OK guv,' he said, and wheeled the car round the approach road, leaving the motorway stretching out behind them.

'Splendid,' said Antick as the car swung back towards Banting. 'It is important, you see, that I make a statement. Tell me, have you been driving taxis for long?'

The *Sparkle!* readers climbed disconsolately back into the coach. They were disappointed because Gavin Jarvis had disappeared without signing any autographs and because they had not had an opportunity to discuss their own writing with the judges as the magazine had promised. They sat in the coach, scowling and muttering to each other as Madge Driller stood by the driver and counted their heads. 'One short,' she said, smiling furiously at them. 'Where is the missing reader?'

But none of her companions had any idea. 'Our dead-line is five,' said Madge Driller, who had assumed responsibility for the readers because of the disturbing events of the afternoon. 'We must leave without her.' The coach pulled out of the car park and the *Sparkle!* readers stared out over the industrial units and the fields where frost was already hardening the earth. As the coach gathered speed one of the readers imagined that she recognised a figure walking slowly in the deep-ening shadows at the side of the road, but it was impos-sible to see clearly in the dark. They discussed the afternoon with a sense of grievance. At the back of the coach one of the readers said that she had seen Gavin Jarvis leaving with the missing member of the party on the back of his motor bike, but none of the others could bring herself to believe it.

'Everyone knows that Eva and I are on the verge of divorce,' said Dove, in the front seat of Morning Pas-time's little car. 'We simply married too young. Many people do and, of course, they change. Everyone changes as they grow older. Eva and I have become two very different people.'

'What you need is a drink,' said Snapper. 'Something to steady your nerves.'

'You're right,' said Dove. 'I feel as if I'm on the edge of a breakdown. Have they done everything they can for Antick?'

'We're not responsible for him.'

'Am I my brother's keeper?'

'Am I Violet's keeper?'

'Of course not. No one could expect you to be.'

'That's right.'

'Of course it is.'

The car accelerated, illuminating for a brief moment the solitary figure of Eddie Rosemary still engaged upon his long walk back to the centre of Banting. For an instant he was clear before them, outlined in the headlights of the car, then he was engulfed in darkness. Neither Dove

169

nor Snapper noticed him as the car shot past. Morning Pastime turned back to see if she had really seen Rosemary walking down the frosty road but there was no one there. She smiled silently, revealing a row of slightly imperfect teeth.

At Banting police station Antick strode up to the desk sergeant in a confident manner.

'Good evening,' he said. 'I have come to report a blackmailer to you, whose identity I have recently discovered. I shall come to his name in a moment. It may be – admittedly a remote possibility – but it may be that you have heard of him. He used to be quite well known for a short time after the war. He has persecuted me for several months now and I have incontrovertible proof of his identity. Please equip yourself with pen and paper.'

The policeman regarded Antick with an air of weariness. The taxi driver who had accompanied him inside spoke up encouragingly. 'This old gent has cracked his identity,' he said, 'through the handwriting and verbal clues.'

'The colour of the ink was the final clue,' said Antick. 'Violet. Purple. You see it was exactly the same colour which he used to sign the letters.'

The policeman stared at them.

'Of course, my local force are already investigating the case,' said Antick, 'but this is a matter of some urgency since I have his speech in my possession. I thought I should come to you straight away.'

'We were doing at least sixty towards the motorway,' said the taxi driver, 'when he raps me one right across the shoulders. Because of the urgency, you see, of his discovery.'

'Now,' said Antick, 'as I have said, you will want pen and paper to take down the details. And I daresay my friend here would welcome a cup of tea.'

'I feel,' said Desmond Bysouth, 'that we have sanitised the arts. We have made them tame, wholesome, good for

170

people, like a dose of tonic or Vitamin C. We have stamped them with official respectability and there is no place in the world any more for people like me.'

He was sitting in the lounge bar of The Rougemont, the large and comfortable hotel in the centre of Banting where Bacon had wanted to hold the judging ceremony. Adrian and Nina listened to him politely.

'Do you write yourself, dear?' Adrian asked her.

'I have written a profile of the winning poet. I am a journalist. I have had rather a demoralising day.'

'Whisky is what you need,' said Bysouth. 'My friend Adrian will oblige.'

'Oh, do let me,' said Nina Cleverly.

'Right you are,' said Bysouth.

'That's really nice of you,' said Adrian.

'I expect it's on expenses,' said Bysouth. 'Journalists never pay for anything, do they?'

'I shall claim heavily for this afternoon,' said Nina Cleverly. 'I agree that we rarely pay for things which cost other people a fortune.'

'Meals, drinks, theatre tickets, holidays,' said Bysouth. 'It must be a wonderful life.'

'Two doubles?'

'Very good of you.'

Nina went to the bar to fetch them.

'Cheers,' said Adrian.

'I enjoyed your speech,' Nina said to Bysouth. 'I thought it very instructive and original.'

'I told him it was really fantastic.'

Bysouth leaned forward. 'You liked the speech?'

'Very much.'

'What did you like most about it?'

'I think your refreshing lack of humility towards the audience.'

'And the judges.'

'Yes, certainly the judges.'

'You liked the argument?'

'I thought it was very forceful.'

'By God it was,' said Bysouth. 'It was forceful all right.'

Nina Cleverly drank some whisky, although she did not like it very much. Then she said: 'Did you send your poem in just for the money?'

Bysouth narrowed his eyes. He looked at her suspiciously, then his face darkened. He was so close to her that she could see the orange stubble of his beard and the black pores that covered his nose.

'What do you mean?'

'Did you send your own poem in for the cash?'

'The poem was sent in by J. W. Blanks.'

'But he doesn't exist.'

'Of course he doesn't exist.'

'He is you.'

'Yes.'

'You sent the poem in.'

'Yes.'

'And no one knows.'

'No.'

'Why did you do it?'

Bysouth drained his glass. 'I am a poet and a genius,' he said. 'I have no need to answer to the conventional moral standards of the day. It is only second-rate intellects who have to account for themselves; I simply live my life and set the rules for others to follow. Call me a monster if you like. Look at my work. That is the testimony on which you should indict me. Besides, I needed the money.'

'Are you going to do it again?'

'I might,' said Bysouth uneasily. 'I could cut you in for a percentage of the profits if you wanted to cooperate in the scheme. Meanwhile I advise you to give up your job as a journalist immediately. It is the occupation of those inferior minds who make it their task to criticise people like me.'

Adrian tapped him on the shoulder. 'Keep your voice down, sweetie. There's Gavin Jarvis.'

'What's he doing here?' said Bysouth. 'That posturing nancy boy.'

'His television series is very successful,' said Nina Cleverly.

'What series?'

' "Poets in a Landscape".'

' "Poets in Landscape"?' shouted Bysouth. 'Poets in a coal mine, poets on a slag heap, what does it matter where they are? It's words, words, words that matter to me.'

'The programme's won critical acclaim.'

'That proves it's no good. Those programmes are just an excuse for people like Jarvis to go off all over the world travelling first class on aeroplanes, all expenses paid.'

Nina saw that Gavin Jarvis was accompanied by the missing *Sparkle!* reader. She was wearing a full, dark skirt and a white blouse with a lace collar. She was young and pretty. Jarvis bought them both drinks, then sat down with her in the far corner of the bar. He put his hand on her thigh and looked sternly into her face, trying to ignore the presence of Bysouth. After a few moments he started to stroke the back of her neck.

'What we need is some entertainment,' said Bysouth. 'A bit of a party. The night is still young.'

'Hardly started,' said Adrian.

'What goes on in this town? What's the night life like?'

'I should think there is very little of it.'

'Nonsense. There will be something going on some-where. We will consult with the management.'

'Super idea,' said Adrian. 'We'll ask the natives.'

Nina Cleverly brought them both two more large whiskies.

'We'll find the "in" place,' said Bysouth. 'Trust us. We always do.'

Adrian got up with difficulty. 'Back in a moment,' he said. 'Be good.'

'Terribly brave,' said Bysouth, gazing after him. 'Terribly brave and terribly proud. One can do nothing for him. It must cause him a great deal of pain but there's nothing he hates more than sympathy. He has a will of iron, a determination of steel.'

'What happened? Did he have an accident?'

'The war,' said Bysouth. 'He was one of its casualties. Horribly shot up. He's blacked it all out of his mind now, can't bear to talk about it. Don't mention a word I've told you.'

'Of course not. I wouldn't dream of it.'

'That's it,' said Bysouth. 'Look at that poseur in the corner crushing that poor young woman to death. On and on, talking about himself, of course. She looks quite a pretty little girl. Far too good for someone like Gavin Jarvis.'

Nina watched him grin and wink at the *Sparkle!* reader.

'Shall I go over and lay seige to her ruby lips?'

'I don't think you should just now.'

'You're probably right. Tell me, what do you know about a man of prurient habits called Bacon?'

There was certainly more than a hint of alcohol on Howard Antick's breath. But this alone would not have deterred the desk sergeant from making his report, had not Antick suddenly become confused while describing the nature of his fourteen previous letters and unable to speak for several minutes. While the taxi driver and the policeman regarded him patiently, a blood vessel in Antick's brain ruptured causing slight paralysis down his right side. Antick continued to explain his letters, but he had some difficulty in forming his words and his movements were uncoordinated. 'The letter –' he kept trying to say, but the words would not form properly and he became incoherent.

The policeman put away his notebook and looked at the taxi driver.

'A drop too much,' he said, 'for our friend here.'

The taxi driver was relieved. 'I couldn't help smelling his breath in the taxi. Pretty strong, if you want my opinion. He'd been to a party and the excitement was too much for him.'

'Now then, sir,' said the policeman, 'do you want to go home quietly with your taxi friend here, or do you want to cause us all a lot of bother?'

Frustratedly trying to form his words, Antick lost his temper and struck the policeman hard with his stick.

The taxi driver laughed. 'He's a real wild gent. He tried that on me in the taxi. There was a nasty look in his eye. He gets vicious in drink, if you ask me.'

'Terrible to see in a man his age,' said the policeman. He came out from behind his desk and took hold of Antick's arm. 'Now then, sir, you come along quietly with me,' he said, 'and we'll book you for assaulting a police officer.'

With staggering steps Antick fought to shake off the officer's grasp but it was useless. With increasing panic he struggled to speak but the words would not come. Incoherent and amazed, Antick gave himself up to the might of superior force. The policeman led him down to the cells where he was placed on a narrow bed and told not to be a nuisance.

Several hours later someone brought him a cup of tea when it was discovered – with some alarm – that the elderly poet was quite unable to drink it.

The railway station was even further than Eddie Rosemary had remembered. In the freezing night he walked quickly to keep warm, despairing of ever seeing the cheerful red and white sign that announced Banting station, and the chance of leaving the hateful town behind. But when he eventually walked into the booking hall it was later than he had thought and he was surprised to see no one there at all. Rosemary looked inside a small wooden hut on the platform and discovered a porter crouched over a glowing electric fire. To his dismay he discovered that there were no trains to London until the following morning since the government had curtailed the service.

'No more trains?' said Rosemary. 'Nothing to London?' But the porter was adamant. Rosemary left the station and wondered where to go. He might try and hitch a lift on the motorway but he could not endure the thought of talking to anyone all the way back to the city.

175

He supposed that the judges and their friends had left Banting long ago and his heart sank again as he thought of their cold, hard faces. Perhaps he could find a cheap bed and breakfast where he could spend the night and catch an early train next morning. Then he remembered that he was now rich; he had been given a cheque for £5000. He would stay in the best hotel at least they owed him that.

Wearily, Rosemary clutched his briefcase and began to walk from the station towards the town centre.

'They say we've come to the right place,' said Adrian, coming back with an air of triumph. 'I've had a long chat with the manager. He was very helpful.'

'What did he say? Tell us the glad tidings,' said Bysouth.

'This is the place to be. There is a disco here every Saturday night. Everyone comes to it.'

'Here?'

'It's called the Rougemont Dine and Dance. I've brought a leaflet.' He showed them a small print sheet advertising the hotel's weekly social night. It said: 'Relax to the sounds of the Groovin' Brothers. Three-course dinner and swinging sounds. Dress, formal. No denim.'

Bysouth stared at the leaflet doubtfully. 'Are you sure this is the sort of thing we want? It looks a bit dull to me.'

'Well what do you expect?' said Adrian petulantly. 'There's nothing else on, so please yourself. You can't expect to find the same as London in a place like this.'

'Should we buy tickets?'

'Five pounds each,' said Adrian. 'If you ask me it's a bargain.'

'I am persuaded,' said Bysouth. He turned to Nina Cleverly. 'I hope that you will do us the honour of joining us for the Dine and Dance?'

'But what about getting home? I expect the last train has gone by now.'

'Adrian and I will be delighted to escort you home in our small but highly reliable car.'

'Thank you.'

'The honour is ours,' said Bysouth, bowing. 'Now I wonder if the tickets might be charged to your expenses . . .'

At the reception desk of the Rougemont Rosemary asked defiantly for a room. Imagining glances of disdain, he spoke quickly and loudly.

'Any luggage?' they asked him.

'Only my briefcase,' said Rosemary, waving it. 'I'm just passing through. An unexpected change of plan.'

'We must ask you to pay now, sir.'

'Pay, yes, fair enough,' said Rosemary, throwing notes over the counter. Everywhere he saw couples standing together. Everyone, it seemed, was linked by indissoluble bonds to another creature.

'The porter will show you to your room.'

'No need,' said Rosemary, seizing the key. 'I can manage quite well alone.'

In the hotel ballroom chairs had been arranged round the perimeter of the room forming a rectangle. Some middle-aged men in tight-fitting black trousers and flowered pink shirts were assembling a collection of instruments and electric wires on the stage. On the side of the drum, pink fluorescent letters proclaimed the Groovin' Brothers. At intervals the oldest-looking Brother would hold the microphone and say, 'Testing, testing, one two three four.' While he spoke, harsh, high-pitched shrieking noises filled the ballroom.

'This looks exciting,' said Bysouth. 'Things are hotting up.' They had finished their three-course meal although Bysouth had very little patience. Through dinner his condition had deteriorated.

'He likes a bit of night life,' Adrian said to Nina. 'He doesn't get out much these days, poor love.'

'Poor old Vi,' said Bysouth. 'If only she was here, eh, Adrian? The silly girl. God knows why she missed the train. Vi always liked a bit of excitement, you know, Nina. She was a very lively girl once.'

Nina Cleverly remembered the middle-aged woman slumped across the table at the Green Carnation but said nothing.

'The trouble with women,' said Bysouth, 'is that they cannot sustain their capacity for excitement. Once Violet liked a good time. Then it all went rotten. She went serious, she started complaining, she nagged. That's no good for a writer. No good for a poet to have someone complaining all the time at you for not paying bills or drinking too much. I'd come home in the afternoon and Vi would start whining about the bills and the flat, so . . .' Bysouth spread his hands wide in a gesture of regret. 'Still, she had her moments, bless her. Do you know Adrian, I think I'll give her a ring.'

Bysouth staggered out of the ballroom and Nina and Adrian sat down in a corner.

'He's still devoted to her,' said Adrian. 'He's such a loyal person. Desmond never forgets a friend.'

'That's marvellous,' said Nina.

Adrian looked at her over the top of his glass. 'Yes,' he said. 'Yes, it really is marvellous.'

Out in the reception lobby Bysouth tried to thrust his coin into the public telephone box. 'Hello, hello,' he shouted. 'Violet is that you?'

But there was nothing except the repeated ringing tone. For as the telephone rang inside her flat Violet lay quietly, submerged in vivid, hallucinatory dreams induced by a combination of vodka and powerful sleeping pills. Lying outstretched in her pungent, dusty bedroom she lay still on the pillows, a glass of vodka near her hand. At the other side of the bed a cigarette smouldered merrily, its glowing embers creating a sparkling combustion with the nylon fibres of the counterpane. A delicate, almost invisible yet acrid column of smoke spiralled upwards into the stale air.

'Hello, hello?' shouted Bysouth. There was no answer. 'Damn,' he said, coming back into the ballroom. 'The machine has swallowed the money. I shall complain to the management.'

'Was Violet there?'

'I'll try later. She would have enjoyed the evening.'

The ballroom became more crowded and the Groovin' Brothers struck up a lively rendering of 'My Way'.

'Things are looking up,' said Bysouth.

'I've never heard the song played like that before,' said Adrian. 'Very original.'

'Irresistible,' said Bysouth, waving his arms above his head and clapping. Several of the dancers turned to stare at him. People wandered into the ballroom and sat primly on chairs arranged round the walls. They came mostly in groups and the male members of the parties laughed and joked with each other, ignoring their wives and girl-friends. They were elaborately dressed in fashions which had not been seen in London for several years. There was no trace of denim.

'They're a bit on the old side, don't you think?' said Bysouth, watching a middle-aged couple dancing.

'Nonsense. They're all younger than you are Desmond.'

'In a very real sense they are all infinitely older, never-theless,' said Bysouth. 'To think that life goes on outside London.'

The Groovin' Brother at the piano took the micro-phone.

'Good evening ladies and gentlemen,' he said softly. His amplified voice rang round the ballroom. 'We're here tonight to make sure you have a wonderful time and leave all your troubles behind you. We want you all to join us here on the floor for our first Rougemont medley and may I remind you all we're happy to play any request you might have for that special song that means so much to both of you.'

The drummer gave a tremendous crash on his drums and the Brothers swung into action.

'*Oh, what a night!*' crooned the singer. '*What a night!*'

The guitarist set up a throbbing accompaniment and several couples stepped self-consciously out onto the floor, moving in small, nervous circles.

'*Oh, what a night! What a night!*'

'Yes,' shouted Bysouth. 'Come along, Nina, we must make our début on the floor.'

'Do you think we should?' she said as Bysouth extended his hand.

'Courage!' he shouted and dragged her onto her feet and into the centre of the polished floor.

The band launched into a medley of popular hits and several more couples joined them.

'Watch out!' cried Bysouth, leading her away from the crowd with a series of quick, fantastic steps that dragged her along in his wake. Once they had enough space to themselves he relinquished his grip of her and began to dance in a primitive but rhythmic manner, flinging his arms to each side and shaking his hips backwards and forwards. Nina Cleverly attempted to match his outlandish movements as the band swayed and smiled and the music grew louder.

'Ah ha!' shouted Bysouth, leaping into the air. 'This is it, Nina. Now we're away.'

Several of the dancers moved away from him.

'Nina,' he shouted above the rhythm of the electric organ, 'can I ask you a favour?'

'Yes.'

'It's Adrian. Would you ask him for a dance when you get back.'

'Yes, if you like.'

'I know what you're thinking,' gasped Bysouth, still jerking to the music though a little less vigorously now. 'It's true he can't dance – at least he can't do this sort of thing – but he would be mortally upset and disappointed, completely cast down if you didn't ask him. He is conscious of his impediment.'

'I'll ask him then.'

'Good girl. I knew you would.'

The Groovin' Brothers began another popular number. Bysouth stopped jerking and swayed from one foot to another. Then he said, 'Would you mind if we went and sat down, just till I get my breath back?'

They left the slowly revolving dancers and joined Adrian at the perimeter.

'That was fantastic,' Adrian said warmly. 'I didn't know you could dance like that, Desmond.'

Bysouth's lips parted in a grin. 'I can still do a lot of things, Adrian,' he said. 'By God, yes.'

Nina Cleverly cleared her throat. 'I wondered if you'd like a dance, Adrian?'

'Oh, how sweet of you. Perhaps a bit later.'

'All right.'

'Thank you for asking.'

Nina Cleverly saw Gavin Jarvis come into the ballroom. He was rather flushed and the *Sparkle!* reader was nowhere to be seen.

'Look, there's our nancy friend again,' said Bysouth. 'Come to sneer at everyone I suppose. I wonder what he's done with his girlfriend. Rather a pretty little thing, I thought.'

'Bit of a tart,' said Adrian.

'He seems to be alone,' said Nina. 'Would you say Jarvis is attractive?'

Adrian studied him with concentration. 'Well, he's not my type, a bit too butch for me, but women might like that sort of thing.'

Bysouth stared gloomily at Jarvis. 'I'm going to phone Violet again. I think she'll be there now.' He left the ballroom again.

'Don't let Desmond upset you, dear,' said Adrian. 'He's had one too many.'

'The day has been too much for him. With all the excitement of the ceremony.'

'You did think his speech was good, didn't you?'

'Yes, I did.'

'You really think so?'

'Yes.'

'You're not just saying that?'

'No, I thought it was very good indeed.'

'It was, wasn't it,' said Adrian, smiling with satisfaction.

A small crowd gathered round Bysouth as he stood in the entrance lobby shouting into the phone. His voice cracked with rage and he banged down the apparatus with a red, shaking hand. A stream of obscenities poured from his lips.

'It must be a wrong number,' someone said in the crowd. Bysouth's torrent of invective continued. The crowd gazed at him in admiration.

As Bysouth swore and cursed flames were now licking cheerfully at the foot of Violet's bed, charring the lower shelves of Alan's Georgian bookcase and his first editions of Thomas Hardy. Soon the curtains caught fire and black smoke began to pour from the bedroom and through the door down the hall corridor. Insensible to the smoke, Violet Glasspool lay peacefully on the bed in a dream-ridden sleep from which she would never wake. The smoke spread into the kitchen and the good, oak wardrobe began to spit and crackle.

'Actually,' said Adrian, 'you may have noticed that I have a wooden leg. That sweet man called Bacon was very sympathetic about it. I suppose you wonder how it happened?'

Uneasily Nina Cleverly smiled at him.

'Well, most people assume it was the war, but that isn't the case, although I sometimes let people think it. No, the truth is that I was knocked down by a BBC messenger on a motor bike when I was crossing the road outside Broadcasting House some years ago. I was dragged quite a long way along the road by the bike and my leg was absolutely mangled. They had to take it off. Funnily enough the bike was delivering one of Desmond's poems for a programme I was producing that evening. That's how I got to know him.'

'I'm terribly sorry.'

'Oh, that's all right,' said Adrian. 'Of course, it has changed my life. Women – well, you can imagine. They regard it as a –'

'Yes, I can imagine,' said Nina hastily.

'But the fact is that it doesn't stop me from getting about. I can do most things.'

'That's marvellous.'

After a short pause, Adrian said, 'I expect you're wondering about Desmond and me.'

'Not at all. I'm sure that's your own affair.'

'Well, I'll tell you. Ever since the accident, when Desmond's poem was arriving on the bike, we have been –'

'The phone's on the bloody blink,' said Bysouth, rejoining them. 'Don't know where the hell she is. Poor old Vi. She was really a good girl, old Vi.' And large tears began to run down the poet's cheeks.

'We've been having a nice chat,' said Adrian.

'Vi, Vi,' cried Bysouth.

'He's rather upset.'

'He'll be all right.'

'Vi, you're a good girl, my little Vi, my little Violet,' said Bysouth, his face now wet with tears.

The room was stuffy and far too hot and the windows would not open. Rosemary sat on the bed and stared at the orange counterpane, the brown and orange curtains and the yellow bedside lamp. There was a distant murmuring in his ears like the hum of machinery that could not be switched off as the sounds of the Groovin' Brothers floated in through the thin bedroom walls. Slowly he opened his briefcase and took out his account journal, his copy of *Advance* and his unused camera.

He turned over the pages of *Advance* and tried to concentrate on an article about the latest developments in New Zealand poetry, but his head ached and his eyes were tired. He looked miserably round the stifling room and went to the window. He looked out at the dull street where the light from a fish and chip shop shone out some twenty yards away. There was a queue in the doorway. Lumpen people were coming away with greasy newspaper parcels, talking in loud, ignorant voices and laughing. Rosemary remembered that he had had no supper and felt his strength ebb away through hunger. But as he watched the servile creatures waiting to be fed he had no appetite for food. Like a god he surveyed them and cast his curses down upon them. He went to the wash basin and poured a glass of water. Then he opened the drawers under the glass-topped dressing table although he had nothing to unpack.

In one of the drawers he found a copy of the Bible, thoughtfully put there by a Gideon for use in time of need. Rosemary imagined the Gideon softly entering the hotel, a suitcase full of Bibles in his hand, moving tactfully along the corridors, placing the books with reverence in an empty drawer. He put the Bible on the bedside table on top of a stained mat bearing the mark of someone else's cup of tea or whisky or false teeth. *Needing sleep*, he read, consulting the index. *Failure comes, Bitter or critical.* He turned to *Anxious or worried*:

When thou passest through the waters, I will be with thee; and through the rivers, they shall not overflow thee: when thou walkest through the fire, thou shalt not be burned; neither shall the flame kindle upon thee . . .

But he could read no further. His eyes filled with tears as despair overwhelmed him.

In the ballroom the dancers were holding each other more closely. Bysouth was horizontal, laid across the length of three chairs by Adrian who seemed accustomed to handling him in such a condition. Nina Cleverly wondered if they would go back to London that night. It seemed of little importance.

The Groovin' Brothers played with passion. The pianist sang throatily into the microphone.

'What about a dance?' said Adrian.

'Will Desmond be all right?'

'He'll be fine. We can just leave him here like this for a bit.'

They advanced awkwardly onto the floor.

'I'm afraid I'm not very good at this sort of thing,' said Adrian. 'I'll just follow you, shall I?'

'If you like.'

'Isn't this a scream?'

'Yes.'

Linked together like beasts in some strange coupling they moved together at the edge of the dance floor. The music came to an end.

'Ta very much,' said Adrian, giggling.

'Thank you.'

They returned to their seats to find that Bysouth had disappeared. The row of chairs was quite empty.

'He won't have gone far, the silly boy,' said Adrian. 'I'll go and look in the bar.'

He stamped out through the dancers. Nina Cleverly stared at her whisky glass.

'I suppose you want me to go and get you another?' She looked up and saw Gavin Jarvis standing beside her, swaying slightly.

'Not particularly.'

He sat down beside her. 'Have we met?'

'At the poetry judging.'

'Right.'

After a few moments he said, 'Do you read women's magazines?'

'No.'

'Great. Do you write poetry?'

'No, I don't.'

'Do you want to know where I get my ideas from?'

'Not really.'

'Do you know who I am?'

'Certainly. I have just written an article which mentions you as one of our leading younger poets.'

'Did you interview me?'

'I'm afraid not.'

'Silly girl,' said Jarvis, and he put one arm round her shoulder. 'I'd have given you a long interview if you'd asked me.'

'Space was limited.'

'I'm on the television,' said Jarvis. 'I'm famous. Why don't you interview me now?' He began to kiss the back of her neck. She wondered what had happened to Adrian and Bysouth.

'*Just let yourself go,*' sang the Groovin' Brothers.
'*Tonight is the time, the right time,*
To say yes, forget about no-o-o . . .'

The street lights threw an orange glare into Rosemary's
bedroom, enriching the glow of the chrysanthemums on
the wallpaper. It was after midnight and somewhere
beyond the haze of the lights stars were visible, but only
to those who looked at them from woods, or fields or
dark, solitary places. Rosemary lay quietly counting the
leaves on the chrysanthemums. In the distance he could
hear a train passing and he wondered if it was bound for
London after all. The water in the pipes of the wash-
basin suddenly gurgled and belched as someone cleaned
their teeth or ran a glass of water. From the bedroom
next door he heard several thumping noises and then the
unmistakeable moans and gasps of persons in bed
together. It was a horrible noise. Rosemary covered his
ears but he could still hear the strange, inhuman sounds.
Acutely aware of his solitude in the hard, cold bed he
prayed that the couple would stop making noises and lay
patiently waiting for sleep. But the groans continued
and sleep would not come. He stared at the tawdry bedroom and it seemed to him that he was the only person
who had ever suffered in all the world.

In the room next door Gavin Jarvis lay heavily on top of
Nina Cleverly. He made loud, grunting cries and spread
heavy limbs over her. Somehow they fell noisily from the
bed to the floor. Nina earnestly hoped that there was no
one in the next room. Her perceptions became horizontal. She saw the orange glow of the street lamp. Jarvis's
breath was strong and his hair luxuriant. He blended
into the darkness and became a strange, unknown creature in the unfriendly night. He was powerful and noisy
and she was pinioned beneath him. Eventually Jarvis
rose unsteadily to his knees, then he gained his feet.

'Must have a pee,' he said, and wandered into the
adjoining room. He was gone for some time. Lying

supine, Nina Cleverly felt the cold night air begin to chill her body and wondered how long Jarvis would be. After some time she got up and sat on the edge of the bed. There was no sound from the bathroom. Fearfully she advanced to the door and pushed it gently. It remained shut. She pushed a little harder and it swung open to reveal Jarvis lying prone at the foot of the lavatory, his breathing stertorous. As she looked into his face, he spoke incoherently and turned away, embracing the pedestal. He was quite insensible. She tried to drag him into the bedroom but his weight was too much for her. After some moments she returned to the bed, where she sank into a troubled sleep as the Groovin' Brothers in the ballroom below began to pack up their instruments.

As Eddie Rosemary heard the Banting parish church clock strike two, a group of people gathered outside a mansion flat in West London to see fire engines with flashing blue lights draw up in an urgent convoy. With heavy hoses firemen burst through the polished wooden doors as gusts of brown smoke burst through a fourth-floor window. Residents of the mansion block, alerted to the danger, were standing tremulous and hysterical in their night clothes, describing to anyone who would listen their sense of shock and terror when they discovered that someone had set their block on fire.

'How many in Flat Twelve?' shouted a fireman. 'How many occupants?'

'Violet Glasspool,' said an elderly woman.

'Anyone else?'

'Well, I don't want to gossip but . . .'

'Is she on her own?'

'Well, to be honest we haven't seen her husband for several months now. He's gone for good, if you ask me.'

'Just the one then?'

'Yes, just the one.'

The firemen rushed up the stairs, through the choking, brown smoke to Violet's securely bolted front door. But though they salvaged the property, they were unable to save Violet Glasspool, whose charred body was later brought out by firemen and delivered to the appropriate authorities. A number of valuable antique books were burned in the fire and quantities of papers. It was rumoured that a great many gin and vodka bottles were discovered in the kitchen cupboards.

12

The news of Violet's death shook them all very badly. Some of her friends blamed Alan Snapper for deserting her, but it was generally agreed that she had been in a bad way for some time.

In the Banjo Club there was an air of despondency.

'They say,' said Bysouth, blinking fiercely, 'that she set the bed on fire. Awful shame. Bloody tragedy.'

'How old was she?' said Adrian.

'Forty-five. Looked it too. She drank too much. I noticed when we had lunch together that day she was pouring it down like water.'

'She missed Alan.'

'He wants his balls kicked in.'

'You can't blame him, poor love.'

Bysouth nodded. 'Not his fault if she starts taking the gin bottle to bed with her.'

'Poor Violet.'

'Couldn't keep a man. She lost two, both her own fault. Men don't like to see a woman drunk; it's a fearful sight.'

'How has Alan taken it?'

'Badly. He's moved into a flat with some blonde. He's very cut up about the whole thing.'

'What a tragedy.'

'Yes,' said Bysouth. 'The fact is, it's thrown me a bit off course, financially speaking. Plans have come adrift. My anticipated income has been laid waste. I am faced with a serious lack of funds. This could be serious.'

He retired to a quieter corner of the club to compose another anonymous letter to Hubert Bacon, increasing the ransom payments to £1000. But, however he calculated it, Bacon's cheques would never compensate him for the potential prize money which he could not hope to win now that Violet had so inconsiderately died. As he wrote, Bysouth was overcome with compunction, to the extent that he sent a note to Howard Antick at his nursing home in Deal, telling him the news of Violet's death. This note was written in violet ink, which Bysouth found movingly appropriate. *There have been differences between us*, he wrote, *but I felt that as one of the old crowd and as a friend of Vi that you would like to know of her misfortune. The funeral is private, but I speak for Snapper in saying you would be most welcome to attend . . .*

Antick received the letter the next day and it was read out to him by one of the nurses. Bysouth's invitation was, after all, fruitless since Antick was unable to leave his bed having lost all coordination and response down the right side of his body. The left side, however, continued to function and although it could not activate the motor muscles upon which speed depended, nevertheless Antick struggled and gurgled, trying to point out to the nurses that the violet ink once again exactly corresponded to the signature of the blackmailing letters. Unfortunately none of the elderly poet's agitation was visible except for the rapid movement of his left eyebrow. They read Bysouth's letter to him again and poured orange juice into his mouth from a special cup. They gave him some powerful sedative drugs and observed that he could not understand what they were saying to him, which was lucky since the news of his friend's death would have upset him dreadfully. Of course, there was no question of his going to the funeral: they arranged to send flowers on his behalf.

'It's tragedy,' said Walter Dove to Eva Vandriver as they sat at their kitchen table sharing a bottle of wine. They had decided to try and make their marriage work once again for the sake of the children. Under some strain, they faced each other over the red burgundy and attempted normal conversation.

'What a terrible way to die. What a tragedy for Violet, and of course for Alan,' said Dove. 'You know, I feel terribly guilty that I didn't do more.'

'What could you have done?' said Eva Vandriver. 'You didn't know her very well, did you?'

'Oh yes, quite well. I feel I could have, in some way, helped her. Quite clearly she was going through a difficult time. Perhaps I could have published more of her poems in *Advance*.'

'She wasn't writing much lately.'

'Well, no she wasn't. She sent me a few poems recently but they just weren't good enough to print. If I had perhaps put just the one in to encourage her . . . If only one had done more. In some sense I feel somewhat to blame.'

Gavin Jarvis rang up the BBC.

'I've had a rather refreshing idea for a programme,' he said. 'A sequel to "Poets in a Landscape". I think this will grab you. We'll call it "A Song of Women" and examine the work of contemporary women poets. We could start with Violet Glasspool who was burned to death the other day. I personally found most of her work resoundingly bathetic though quirkily authentic for her age and class, but we could say it was time for a re-evaluation. It would be a good peg for the series. Look, why don't we talk this through lunch? Next week? OK, that would be great.'

'It is,' said Bacon, dictating to Cheryl, 'a very great tragedy and on behalf of the company we would like to express our most sincere sympathy . . .'

He had been asked by the chairman to send a personal letter as a mark of respect. Bacon felt the horror of it deeply. She had been lying there, slumped and unconscious, while they had laughed and drunk champagne at Banting and joked about her failure to appear. How he hated those dreadful poets with their wretched, disorganised lives. Bacon paused in his dictation and looked at his watch. He would have to leave earlier than usual to make another deposit at Waterloo station. Doreen would be furious if he missed his usual train. Another anonymous letter had come for him that morning. They would not stop now, Bacon knew, until he was completely bankrupt, his life's savings exhausted. Like Violet, his life was in ruins. His prospects were extinguished, the threat of those anonymous letters turning everything to ashes. 'We would like you to know that our admiration for Miss Glasspool was profound and we send our deepest sympathy for the tragic accident which ended her life, still full of promise . . .'

It was as if he was composing his own epitaph.

Violet Glasspool's solicitor visited Madge Driller at the *Sparkle!* offices, spreading out his papers in the suffocating cloud of *Fantôme de l'Opéra*.

'All her money?' said Madge Driller. 'What an extraordinary act of charity. This is quite unexpected. We could not possible accept.'

The terms of Violet's will were explained to her. She had left everything to *Sparkle!*, to further the cause of women's writing. She had asked that a small bequest might be set up, an annual competition perhaps, so that women might explore the artistic potential within them. Madge Driller considered the terms of the Glasspool Bequest.

'I think we might do better to donate the money to a suitable charity, perhaps Alcoholics Anonymous. I would be quite happy to put a discreet announcement in the paper. Of course, we will do everything to further her wishes. I can't imagine why she thought of us.'

But the Glasspool Bequest unfortunately came to nothing when it was discovered that Violet had died leaving debts of over two thousand pounds. *Sparkle!* instead carried a poem by Gavin Jarvis, dedicated to Violet's memory, and engaged him as a monthly columnist.

* * *

Eddie Rosemary telephoned *Sparkle!* House and asked to speak to Nina Cleverly. A strange voice answered her phone.

'Nina Cleverly please,' said Rosemary in agitation. 'I must speak to her urgently about an article she has written about me.'

'She isn't here.'

'I must talk to her about the article. Look, I don't want to complain. She has a right to say anything she likes, even if it wasn't particularly flattering, but that isn't why I telephoned. The fact is that something has gone wrong. There is the most terrible misprint in my poem, second verse, line five. I don't know if you have a copy to hand?'

'You should speak to Miss Cleverly about it.'

'But she isn't there.'

'No, she has gone to interview philosophers at Oxford with Lord Broubster.'

'I don't care where she's gone,' said Rosemary. 'You must see the line I mean. It's not mine. I mean, I did not write it. It is a line of someone else's poem which has got into mine somehow. It is a terrible mistake.'

'Would you like to ring back next week?'

'Do you have a copy there?' said Rosemary. 'You must see that this makes nonsense of the verse. I'm not asking for special treatment. I just want you to print a correction. Obviously the poem can't be left as it is. Do you see the line I mean? "Blonde hair recalled each evening in spaghetti". It just has nothing to do with my poem. I can't think how it got there. Do you see what I mean?'

There was a silence.

'Hello,' said Rosemary. 'Are you still there? Verse two, line five. Hello?'

'Would you like to write a letter to the editor?'

'No,' said Rosemary. 'I want you to look at the poem.'

'I'm afraid I don't know much about poetry.'

He put the telephone down. There was nothing he could do. They would not, he saw now, change the line. They were not interested in his poem. He turned over yesterday's paper, lying unread on the table. 'Woman poet dead in fire,' he read. 'The death was announced yesterday of the noted woman poet, Violet Glasspool, who was found by firemen in the bedroom of her mansion flat in West London after fire swept through her home . . .'

Rosemary stared in disbelief at the paper. Violet Glasspool was dead; his benefactor and patron had been burned to death. 'No,' he whispered. He read the report again. A blurred picture of Violet smiled out from the newspaper, taken in her younger days. Had she looked like that? Rosemary had never seen her face to face. He had never spoken to her. All he had was the letter she had written to him and the promises she had held out.

He dropped the newspaper and went into his bleak sitting room. The promises were gone, destroyed with Violet in the flames. He could not endure it. His hopes of entering the forbidden world, of being accepted and recognised, were over. Rosemary saw the long, lonely years stretching before him. Encouragement, at that particular moment, had been crucial. He had chanced everything on the recognition the competition would bring. And, at the most important hour, he had been denied it.

Some poets, he knew, could risk everything, could gamble with immortality, believing with confidence that they were writing for future generations. But he could not. He did not have the spirit to carry on. He put his head in his hands and closed his eyes. He felt cold and very tired.

When he woke it was morning. Rosemary slowly went up to his study and filled a large shopping bag with pieces of paper, the fragments of his poems, some half-finished, some complete, some mere scrawls of words. Growing enthusiastic, he ransacked his drawers for notebooks, piling them into his bag. He filled two carrier bags with ten years' work, leaving the room in chaos, with overturned drawers and scattered files. It was growing light as Rosemary made the familiar journey

194

down to the motorway, stepping carefully through the thistles and the damp, wet rushes. The air was sharp, and in the grass under his feet he could smell the advance of spring. Clutching his carrier bags he walked slowly down to the tunnel. He had been crying earlier, but now he felt alert and clear-headed. He breathed deeply and, raising his arms, emptied his carrier bags over the earth. Above him, the cars passed in rapid succession. He turned his back on the litter of paper and began to walk towards the railway station.

As Rosemary's train pulled into Paddington a number of poets were arriving at the West London Crematorium for the Celebration of Farewell for Violet Glasspool. Cellophane packages of flowers were displayed in the corridor for the consolation of her friends and relatives. Pausing in awkward groups they read the messages on the small white cards which were attached, bearing the stilted sentiments of regret. There was a bunch of orange gladioli from Howard Antick ordered by the matron of the Deal nursing home and bearing the words: *Sincere condolences in your loss.* Violet's polytechnic students contributed to an ornate wreath which bore the message: *Violet Glasspool, a brilliant teacher and a supportive friend.*

Alan Snapper stood guiltily by the largest bunch – white roses and lilies which Morning Pastime had obligingly ordered from the local florist. His friends repeatedly came up to him and assured him that it was not his fault. There was nothing, they said in soft, low voices, that anyone could have done.

Inside the chapel, they sat quietly, contemplating the red brick walls while a tape recorder emitted the poignant notes of Dido's farewell lament to Carthage. Privately Walter Dove considered the Purcell rather an odd choice, but Snapper told Eva Vandriver that it was one of Violet's favourite pieces.

'She said she wanted it played at her funeral,' he said, 'in the way one talks about these things. I told her I

195

wanted "Sympathy for the Devil" by the Rolling Stones.'

'I'd rather have Bob Dylan,' she said. ' "Mr Tambourine Man", I think. But I hope to God I survive Walter.'

Snapper coughed nervously. 'There was nothing I could have done,' he said to Gavin Jarvis, who was crouching in the pew next to him with a producer from the BBC.

'Right,' said Jarvis. 'We couldn't do anything. She was a very crazy, mixed-up lady.' Jarvis was already hard at work on 'A Song of Women', preparing the programme about Violet's life and work.

'There was nothing any of us could have done,' said Snapper, angrily refusing the burden of guilt.

'No one blames you.'

'Yes they do.'

'It was just one of those things.'

'I think she did it deliberately. You know, as a sort of last gesture of revenge. Of course, she's ruined my life, dying like that. Everyone will always say it was my fault.'

> *'When I am laid, am laid in earth*
> *May my wrongs create,*
> *No trouble, no trouble . . .'*

Dido's lament flooded the air as the mourners sat in gloomy silence.

'An interesting reference to "earth" there,' said Walter Dove. 'Do you think Violet would have preferred to be buried?'

'I've no idea,' said Eva Vandriver. 'I suppose Snapper would know wouldn't he?'

'I suppose he would.'

> *'remember me, remember me*
> *But ah! forget my fate . . .'*

'Anyway, no one is actually buried these days are they? Standing round the grave, watching the coffin go down. It's too horrible.'

'Man that is born of a woman hath but a short time to

live, and is full of misery,' said Dove thoughtfully. 'He cometh up, and is cut down, like a flower – it's interesting isn't it, that we prefer the flames these days to the sombre implications of Cranmer's prose? That might make rather a good subject for an article, don't you think?'

Over the notes of the music there was a sustained muttering from the back of the chapel where Bysouth was talking to himself, reliving the early days of his marriage to Violet. Mournfully he remembered how he and Violet had shared so many bottles of whisky, wasting their early promise and squandering precious time.

The music stopped. A vicar appeared from a side door and said to them, 'I know that Violet would have wished us to think of her today in a spirit of happiness. Although she unfortunately cannot be with us she would want us to rejoice that she is now, at last, set free from her suffering. For death came to her as a merciful release. We who are left will miss her very much. But we should not want her back, since we prefer to remember her happily in the prime of her life.'

'That vicar has made a mistake,' Snapper whispered to Jarvis. 'He's talking about somebody else.'

'Advanced in years as she was,' said the vicar, 'we will think of her frequently as our own lives progress and always be glad to remember her contribution to society.'

'He's confused the order of cremations. Can't somebody tell him he's got it wrong?'

Looking wildly round the chapel, Snapper saw a figure standing near the back conspicuous in a dark suit and a black tie. Where most of Violet's friends had come in their usual unconventional costume, the figure stood sombre and rigid, punctiliously observing the order of service.

'Who is that?' said Snapper.

'No idea,' said Jarvis.

'Perhaps he's one of Violet's students.'

'Doesn't look like a student.'

'His face is vaguely familiar.'

'He's probably one of those professional mourners who

197

go to all the cremations. They are obsessed by morbid fantasies.'

'I hope he isn't going to make a scene.'

'Ignore him.'

'I need a drink,' said Snapper.

'And so,' said the vicar, 'after a long and meaningful life enriched by her gift for inter-personal relationships she has made her transition. But we are pleased and thankful for the experience of knowing such a fine and caring person.'

He pressed a button and the tape recorder started up again as Jarvis stepped out from the congregation to read one of Violet's shorter poems. Climbing up to the rostrum he began to declaim the lines of 'A Waking Wind' as the small coffin shuddered into movement and slowly rolled forward through red velvet curtains which trembled gently after its passing.

Snapper stared at the slightly moving curtains. But Violet's body had long since been consumed by flames.

Eddie Rosemary stood stiffly to attention as the coffin moved out of sight. He considered the manner of her death, alone and perhaps in despair. If only he had met her at Banting. If only they had talked.

The music played on. Gradually the friends of Violet Glasspool left their pews and gathered outside the chapel, rubbing their hands and shuffling their feet on the cold gravel path. Rosemary looked around at the collection of poets who were talking loudly to each other. He saw Bysouth staring hard at the crematorium chimney, waiting for the puff of smoke that would signify the incineration of his former wife. How could he have envied such a person?

Morning Pastime came up to Alan Snapper. Distractedly he patted her bottom.

Jarvis thumped him on the back. 'The show's over,' he said.

'Are you coming to the reception,' asked Snapper.

Jarvis looked at his watch. 'I can give you forty minutes,' he said, 'then I have to get to the heliport. We're flying up to Manchester for a helicopter signing.'

'Helicopter?'

'To promote my new collection, *Anus*. They're going to hover over the civic hall and lower me down on a winch. Great idea. Ties in with the theme.'

'Fantastic,' said Snapper. 'Look –'

He stopped as Eddie Rosemary walked up to him along the gravel path. Nervously he backed away, remembering Jarvis's warning about morbid obsessions.

Rosemary stopped and held out his hand. 'I'm terribly sorry.'

'Have we met?' said Snapper.

'Briefly, at Banting,' said Rosemary. 'I just wanted to say how sorry I am about Miss Glasspool. I was very upset when –' He swallowed as tears threatened to overwhelm him. Snapper looked away in embarrassment.

Walter Dove and Eva Vandriver came up to Snapper. 'Look, Alan,' said Dove in a reverent voice, 'we're giving lifts to the Terpsichore Club. We'll take as many people as we can. Don't worry about transport. You're going with Morning?'

'Yes,' said Snapper.

Eva Vandriver walked down the path a little way with Gavin Jarvis. 'It isn't working,' she said. 'It's hopeless trying to start again, he's not in sympathy with anything I want to do. He's a repressive influence. If it weren't for the children . . .'

'How old is Sophie?' said Jarvis. 'She came to one of my classes at the Porson Institute the other day. She looked older than I remembered.'

'She's only sixteen.'

'Ah,' said Jarvis. 'I thought she was older. She looks older.'

'Look,' said Eva Vandriver. 'Why don't we have a drink some time?'

'Right. Let me call you,' said Jarvis. 'My diary is pretty booked up these days.'

Rosemary said to Snapper. 'She was very helpful to me. I owe her so much. She was . . . very kind.'

199

'By the way,' said Dove. 'I've been meaning to ask you, Alan. Do you think Violet actually wanted to be cremated? You see, the reference in the music was very much to earth. I wondered if she intended, perhaps, some poetic irony between burial and –'

'We couldn't find any of her papers after the fire,' said Snapper. He turned to Rosemary. 'I didn't know you knew her. Of course, she encouraged a great many people.'

'I never knew her,' said Rosemary. 'I hoped I would one day. Now, of course –'

'Come on, mate,' said Jarvis, punching Snapper hard on the shoulder. 'You'll feel better after a drink.'

'Yes. Do you know Mr – er?'

'Rosemary.'

'No,' said Jarvis.

'Yes,' said Rosemary.

'Have we met?' said Jarvis. 'Great, how are you?'

Rosemary stood still as a great anger spread through his body like the flames that had consumed Violet.

'We have met,' he said to Jarvis. 'We have met. Why don't you remember?'

'OK, we've met. Take it easy.'

'We met at Banting, at the Coote & Balding presentation.' As he spoke he remembered his humiliations. 'You judged my work. You gave me a prize. Why don't you remember?'

'That's great,' said Snapper. 'Look, Rosemary, why don't you come along to the Terpsichore Club with us? We're having a small reception, we can give you a lift. Plenty of cars. I'm sure Violet would have wanted you to come.'

'Sure, no problem,' said Jarvis. 'Come along. Good idea.'

Rosemary looked at Violet's friends as they made their way towards the cars. Violet, after all, could not have offered him a passport to the world he longed to join, for that world did not exist. He had made a mistake.

'No,' Rosemary said. Anger shook him. Snapper and Jarvis continued to talk to each other.

'No!' Rosemary shouted.

There was a sudden silence – except for the sound of Bysouth hawking and spitting on the gravel – as everyone turned to look at him.

'I don't want to come with you,' said Rosemary. 'I don't want anything to do with you.'

Suddenly his anger was over. He walked quietly away down the gravel path. They stared after him as he left, but he no longer cared what they thought of him. He caught the train back to Slough. When he reached his house in Appletree Crescent he went to bed and fell immediately into a deep, dreamless sleep.

Violet Glasspool's funeral party lasted for several hours.

'God bless her,' cried Bysouth, emptying a bottle of whisky. 'What a woman! What a wife!'

'She was a wonderful person.'

'A marvellous teacher.'

'Here's to you, Vi, I'll never forget you.'

'Cheers.'

'He's presenting a television programme about her.'

'She had such a distinctive style . . .'

'. . . in a helicopter.'

'. . . sort of shifting and protean.'

'God bless you Vi, my little Violet.'

'. . . a monumental ego.'

'Of course, she married the wrong kind of men . . .'

'. . . what an opportunist.'

'Here's to Violet.'

'To Violet.'

'Rest in peace.'

'Cheers.'

The last guests were staggering away from the Terpsichore Club when Eddie Rosemary woke with a start. He opened his eyes, and stared round his dark bedroom. His navy blue suit lay creased on the floor where he had discarded it. He lay for several minutes

201

thinking about Violet's cremation, then it became clear to him what he must do. He got out of bed and put on his Wellington boots and anorak.

In the torchlight the path under the motorway was strange territory. The usual landmarks of the day were gone as trees, stones and fences took on distorted, deceiving shapes. Shining the torch Rosemary edged forward cautiously through the barbed wire fence, down the sloping field to the area of marshy grass.

He looked up at the sky where Orion was conspicuous among the less familiar stars. In the darkness a steady stream of cars flashed past, rushing to their unknown destinations. Gratefully Rosemary looked up at them. The cars were still there. Nothing had stopped. He shone the torch carefully.

Caught in the tunnel, blown up against the concrete wall, white pages fluttered in the weak light of the torch. Driven against the motorway's solid foundations, his poems stirred a little in the light wind, spreading over the damp grass. The ink was smudged on some of the sheets but most of his words were still legible. After a few moments Rosemary went forward and began to gather them up.

THE END

Noah's Ark
Barbara Trapido

NOAH'S ARK is a wry and sparkling account of a marriage: an apparently incompatible union between Noah Glazer, a solid man of science, and Alison Bobrow, a palely captivating eccentric, who Noah suspects of 'keeping a Tarot Pack in the bureau drawer'. For both the marriage – after a memorably sexy and precipitous courtship implies a serious departure from type. Noah walks undaunted into the overpopulated labyrinth of Alison's life, coolly issuing forth the unspeakable maxim that 'Charity begins at Home'. The result is serenity and order, until Alison is drawn to explore certain avenues in her past. The consequences are both hectic and illuminating. . . .

NOAH'S ARK, with its lively wit, its piquant insight and its varied and outrageous characters, more than fulfils the promise of the prize-winning BROTHER OF THE MORE FAMOUS JACK (also available in Black Swan)

'An achingly funny novel . . . wickedly observed'
LIBBY PURVES, LIVING

'Witty and highly polished . . . never a dull moment'
ALANNAH HOPKIN, THE STANDARD

'Zesty, intelligent and highly readable'
DEBORAH MOGGACH, COSMOPOLITAN

'Reading it is rather like being bombarded by sequins'
ANTHONY THWAITE, THE OBSERVER

0 552 99130 9   £2.95

BLACK SWAN

Brother of the More Famous Jack
Barbara Trapido

'A sort of Bohemian *Brideshead Revisited*'
TIMES LITERARY SUPPLEMENT

Here are the Goldmans: Jacob, born in London's Jewish
ghetto, and now an eminent professor of philosophy, and
wife, Jane, an acid-tongued earth-mother who rocked her
aristocratic family by going off to live with Jacob in
bohemian squalor. We enter their ebullient, untidy world
through Katherine, a student of Jacob's who falls in love
with the oldest Goldman child. When the affair ends badly,
Katherine flees to Rome, determined to put them *all* behind
her. But she returns, ten years later, seasoned and more
knowing, to discover that their lives are inextricably
bound, that old wounds do heal, and that life goes forward
in all its deep and satisfying bounty.

'A wry, elegant and involving novel that introduces a major
new talent to the world of literature.

'I hope it is stocked by railway-station bookstalls. I hope
railway-station bookstalls have to build extensions to house
the necessary copies'
FINANCIAL TIMES

'The style is hectic and passionate, the jokes thick and fast,
the emotions full and right, the humanity total and
engulfing . . . a first fruit to savour and exalt'
THE TIMES

'Its high spirits are irresistible. Like Moll Flanders, the
heroine is unstoppable'
SUNDAY TELEGRAPH

0 552 99056 6   £3.50

BLACK SWAN

Jumping The Queue
Mary Wesley

'A virtuoso performance of guileful plotting, deft
characterization and malicious wit'
THE TIMES

Matilda Poliport, recently widowed, has decided to End It
All. But her meticulously planned bid for graceful oblivion
is foiled, and when later she foils the suicide attempt of
another lost soul – Hugh Warner, on the run from the
police – life begins again for both.

But life also begins to throw up nasty secrets and awkward
questions: just what was Matilda's husband Tom doing in
Paris? How is the soon-to-be-knighted John (or Piers as he
likes to be called) involved? Was Louise more than just a
lovely daughter? And why did Hugh choose Matilda as his
saviour?

Jumping the Queue is a brilliantly written first novel
brimming over with confidence and black humour,
reminiscent of Muriel Spark at her magnificent best.

'Great verve and inventiveness . . . (Matilda is) a
convincing original'
TIMES LITERARY SUPPLEMENT

0 552 99082 5   £1.95

── **BLACK SWAN** ──

The Camomile Lawn
Mary Wesley

'A very good book indeed . . . has the texture and smell of real life,
rich in detail, careful and subtle in observation, mature in
judgement'
SUSAN HILL

'It is hard to overpraise Mary Wesley's novel . . . exceptional grace
and understanding . . . so tingly and spry with life that put a mirror
to the book and I'll almost swear it will mist over with the breath of
the five young cousins'
THE TIMES

Behind the large house, the fragrant camomile lawn stretches
down to the Cornish cliffs. Here, in the dizzying heat of August
1939, five cousins have gathered at their aunt's house for their
annual ritual of a holiday. For most of them, it is the last summer of
their youth, with the heady exhilarations and freedoms of lost
innocence, as well as the fears of the coming war around the
corner.

The Camomile Lawn moves from Cornwall to London and back
again, over the years, telling the stories of the cousins, their family
and their friends, united by shared losses and lovers, by family ties
and the absurd conditions imposed by war as their paths cross and
recross over the years. Mary Wesley presents an extraordinarily
vivid and lively picture of wartime London: the rationing,
imaginatively circumvented; the fallen houses; the parties, the new-
found comforts of sex, the desperate humour of survival – all of it
evoked with warmth, clarity and stunning wit. And through it all,
the cousins and their friends try to hold on to the part of
themselves that laughed and played dangerous games on that
camomile lawn.

'Extraordinarily accomplished and fast-moving . . . plotted with
great deftness and intelligence'
MARTIN SEYMOUR-SMITH, FINANCIAL TIMES

'Nothing old-fashioned or even ladylike about it. With the verve and
jollity of youth . . . a book as scatty and chatty as a gossip column'
MAIL ON SUNDAY

'Delightful . . . wholly believable and exact. I like the mixture of
warmth and wit . . . More, please'
DAILY TELEGRAPH

0 552 99126 0   £3.95

BLACK SWAN

Harnessing Peacocks
Mary Wesley

'Delightful, intelligent entertainment'
THOMAS HINDE, SUNDAY TELEGRAPH

Hebe listens in the darkness of the hall to a family
conference. The stern hypocrisy of her grandfather is
winning the day. He has summoned her three horsey
sisters' successful husbands and they are discussing
Hebe's unexpected pregnancy. The decision, unanimous, is
that it be terminated. Hebe, dissenting, flees into the night.

Twelve summers later she is living happily alone with her
son in a seaside town in Cornwall. He is receiving an
expensive education. Hebe has organised her life oddly but
well. She has two chief talents in life – cooking and making
love – and these she has exercised with dignity, in privacy
and for profit.

It is when the separate strands of the web of Hebe's life
become entangled that the even tenor of her days is
threatened, and her life is changed.

HARNESSING PEACOCKS, Mary Wesley's third novel, is
suffused with freshness, warmth and wit. The author's
delightful literary skills are here fully engaged in a story of
independence, honesty and sensual charm.

'Mary Wesley goes from strength to strength . . . She has a
great zest for life . . . The book is tremendously lively, very
funny, touching, spirited'
SUSAN HILL, GOOD HOUSEKEEPING

0 552 99210 0   £3.95

BLACK SWAN

All Things Nice
Rachel Billington
author of A WOMAN'S AGE

'A sharp and observant eye . . . with its lively evocation of two New Yorks, this is a promising debut'
RICHARD LISTER, EVENING STANDARD

Kate is an innocent abroad – a well-brought-up English girl with impeccable connections, totally unsophisticated, and without an idea in her pretty head. She has come to New York to get away from a mother she can't forgive for her treatment of her alcoholic father. She has a childish dream of becoming a writer.

From her arrival, she is whirled into New York on two levels – Picasso-lined apartments, weekend retreats of the fashionable rich on one – and the welfare of a self-destructive drug addict on the other. During a long summer, Kate's innocence carries her through various encounters almost unscathed, as she tries to reconcile these conflicting worlds – and nearly succeeds.

First published in 1969, and set in the sweet and sour New York of the 1960s, *All Things Nice* portrays Kate's awakening, her progress from visiting English maiden to one intimately caught up in the grinding business of New York survival. Both funny and sad, Rachel Billington's first novel has a vibrant and exceptional style.

'A witty, observant, well mannered piece of writing that I enjoyed from first to last. Lady Rachel has apparently not wasted her time in New York; fellow sufferers and fellow enthusiasts will recognise with evil glee many of the personalities paraded for our amusement . . . I laughed a lot and had my touch of sentiment, and recommended *All Things Nice* as a triumphantly successful novel, doubly remarkable as being a debut'
DOMINIC LE FOE. THE ILLUSTRATED LONDON NEWS

'A sharply intelligent and highly enjoyable look at the high-life of Manhattan'
IAIN HAMILTON, DAILY TELEGRAPH

0 552 99164 3   £3.50

BLACK SWAN